T0301258

SILVERBACK

Also by Phil Harrison

The First Day

SILVERBACK

PHIL HARRISON

FLEET
2024

FLEET

First published in Great Britain in 2024 by Fleet

1 3 5 7 9 10 8 6 4 2

Copyright © 2024 by Phil Harrison

The moral right of the author has been asserted.

A CIP catalogue record for this book
is available from the British Library.

Hardback ISBN 978-0-3497-2797-4
C-format ISBN 978-0-3497-2798-1

Typeset in Bembo by M Rules
Printed and bound in Great Britain by Clays Ltd, Elcograf S.p.A.

Papers used by Fleet are from well-managed forests
and other responsible sources.

Fleet
An imprint of
Little, Brown Book Group
Carmelite House
50 Victoria Embankment
London EC4Y 0DZ

An Hachette UK Company
www.hachette.co.uk

www.littlebrown.co.uk

For Myrid

The bitten tongue tries to lick itself.

Michael Eigen

1

Fechner wondered why he'd been chosen.

He was surrounded now, jury members splayed across two benches, preparing like him to sit in judgement of a fellow man. The courtroom buzzed with anticipatory fervour, appetite. Whispers hustled the air into life, humming with sexual excitement. The little voice ran through him. *You cut bodies open, remove offending parts, close them back up again. You do not need to be here.* Fechner had been told the administration would write him a letter – the importance of his position, the extent of his skills, etcetera. But: civic duty. And why shouldn't he want something new, some intervention to break the stark repetition of his days? He was a man of solitary passions.

Rusting was led in. Confident, shoulders back; no meekness, no supplication. No doubt, thought Fechner, how he would plead. *Who are you to gather here and judge me?* He was prodigious, his body an exaggeration. Menace attended him. His hair, cropped tight to his large head, shone like silk under the harsh lights. His arms were fat balloons, comically bulky. Still there was something boyish about him, in the way he walked, a lithe grace, a furtiveness. He moved as though in slow motion, unhurriable. Rusting looked

1

around, taking it all in, measuring this new space in which he would be paraded, day after day, like an animal.

Fechner felt the rise in his gut, revulsion surely, but not only revulsion. There was a sweetness in it too. They led Rusting to the dock, swore him in. As he sat down, he looked at them for the first time, those who would judge him. Fechner had to stop himself smiling.

Rusting killed his father, or so the prosecution would claim. That was what Fechner and his compatriots were here to decide. It struck Fechner, listening to the judge's outline of what was to come, that the legal truth of this would be determined not by what happened but by what he and his fellow jurors came to decide had happened, an extraordinary situation fraught with power and complex responsibility. Fechner's own sense of the inner workings of guilt was live and vivid.

As a child, Fechner was very close to an uncle, his mother's brother, Abraham, named for the patriarch. Abraham worked as an undertaker on the Newtownards Road, in east Belfast. His skill was in the preparation of a body for burial or cremation. He had a gift, they said, for just the right amount of verisimilitude. A corpse should look like the person, but not too much like the person, lest the difference – life itself – be made to appear meaningless. People must be able to believe, simultaneously, that the body before them both was and was not their loved one. This is no small gift, and his talent afforded him not only a profession but a reputation.

Abraham had a certain dryness of humour to accompany the melancholic bent. Invariably he wore a suit and tie, even when preparing a body late at night for a funeral the following morning. 'Why do you always dress up?' Fechner asked him once, and he answered, straight-faced, 'In case Jesus comes back.' Fechner loved him. When his classmates rushed down to the docks on bikes, or to the Orangefield pitches with a football, he would walk round to McAllisters Funeral Home and watch in silence as skin was brightened, grimaces placated, the dull unresponsive flesh made obedient to the needs of the living.

Fechner had taken to Abraham even as a baby. The family story went that Fechner cooed and gurgled for his uncle like for no other human, a story that Fechner heard often enough from his mother that he supposed it must be true. They had their small friendship over the years, Abraham a largely silent but placid figure around whom Fechner could run and climb and find his feet. It had happened – though Fechner, looking back, could not say how – that the running and climbing had ceased, little by little no doubt, and by the age of nine or ten he had taken on, as though by some sort of spiritual transmission, the characteristics of the older man. Restrained, sensible, not distant exactly, but carefully mannered. Even the surname by which he thought of himself, Fechner – rather than his given name, James – mimicked the way his uncle addressed him.

Abraham by this time allowed him to stay and watch as he worked, occasionally handing him something to hold. After a few months he gave him a small brush and showed him how to clean the fingernails, and Fechner carried out the task perfectly, with hushed, determined precision. A tremendous feeling of satisfaction carried Fechner home that day. As they ate dinner – he, his mother and his father – he glowed with intention.

'What's got into you?' his mother said.

He wanted to tell her, but knew that he would be mocked. He was always weighing this up. 'Credulous', she had called him once, and when he looked the word up it struck him as true. So he said nothing.

The opening statements. William Rusting's body was discovered in a ditch beside the Connswater River. He was

3

wearing a cheap red dress, torn at one shoulder. The silence in the courtroom sharpened as the prosecutors described his last day of life, strolling up the Newtownards Road in heels and lipstick, on his way to perform a Dolly Parton routine at a small social club in east Belfast. The prosecution claimed that Robert Rusting hated this, was embarrassed and ashamed of it, and murdered his father, leaving his body as a warning, as a declaration. Rusting stared straight ahead, unflinching save for the soft outline of his jaw giving ever so slightly at the word 'warning'.

Rusting's counsel was a man called Ingram. He was small, weaselly, with a full head of slicked-back black hair; his hands constantly darted in and out of each other like shy rats. He outlined his intention to show that the claims made by the prosecution were speculative and conjectural. His manner was conciliatory. He did not try to paint a pretty picture. 'It would be an understatement,' he admitted, 'to say that Robert did not get on with his father.' He described his client as difficult, raw, even prone to violence. It struck Fechner as a bold strategy, but he sensed the power in it, the potential. He watched Rusting, blanking at the desk before him, a slick sort of pride heavy on his shoulders. 'It is important to remember,' Ingram continued, addressing the jury directly, 'that you are here to decide if Robert Rusting killed his father, not if you want to be his friend.'

Abraham was long dead now, a heart attack in his fifties while Fechner was still a teenager. In less than a year, his mother had followed: cancer, slow and painful. Fechner had watched her become a sufferer, her body turning against itself. He was helpless, but still the guilt ate away at him, his inability to save her. She had not much enjoyed life, even before the cancer. She used to look at him as a child with

4

what he felt was a sort of regret, and he could never unpick what the regret was for, or how deeply he was implicated in it. It wasn't that she was harsh with him; there was just little affection. There'd been a year – he was six, seven – when he had fought it, drove hard into her, hunting for reactions; love obviously, but by the end even hatred would have done. He got nothing. He was peripheral to her, spectral. Free, in a sense. It was a strange sort of freedom, satisfying as far as it went, but it could never go quite far enough. Or perhaps it would be better to say that in this time he realised that it wasn't freedom he wanted. They went their own ways then. Abraham filled in, to some degree, and Fechner had enough about him to make his way through the minor degradations of school life, the casual cruelties that made up the day, the caustic little authoritarian punishments the teachers meted out, frustrated by their own lack of real power. Mirrored, too, by their imitators among the pupils, fuelled on the same failures. It was politics, navigating that, trying to find yourself, make yourself into something. The Troubles indeed.

When Abraham died, Fechner had gone to see his body in McAllisters and stared at it in mute wonder. The sorrow he felt was blunt, numbing. Remarkable, he thought, how something – someone – could just *end*. But he held himself together, neither grief nor fear getting a grip on him. It was an achievement, of a sort. His mother's death was a closer affair. She returned home after the failed treatments, cried out in pain nightly from her room. He sat with her, held her hand. She seemed to be trying to work herself up to some expressiveness. At moments she would hint at a gesture, draw him in, and then abandon it halfway through, vexed and exhausted. The muscles had atrophied, inside and out. As Abraham had once told him, you do not get out at the end what you do not put in along the way.

Fechner's body – changing dramatically at this time, hair and penis and chest all modifying, mobile – he began to experience as an insult to hers. As though his aliveness was mocking her. He was with her when she died. He watched the breath dissipate, then cease, an emptiness descending on the room. He knew. He stood up and lifted her body in his arms, just to feel the weight of it. It was like lifting a child. He set her back down softly and closed her eyes with his hand. He was disgusted with himself, with the joy he felt.

The first trial day ended around four. The jurors nodded, smiled, shrugged at one another. Strangers no longer, their shared responsibility a form of communion. Fechner was struck by their excitement. Kevin, the youth worker who he'd sat with at lunch, offered his hand. 'Wild, hey?' he said, gleeful. 'See you tomorrow!'

After court finished Fechner had a couple of hours to kill. He went to the gym. From the treadmill he surveyed, as usual, the regulars. He didn't know any of them, not really, just to dip the head on the way past and nod at in encouragement. He was sceptical of the ones who came in to be looked at, but still he looked at them. He moved through his routine – ten minutes on the tread, ten on the cross, ten on the bike. By the final ten, on the rower, he was melting. But this is what he came for. Shifting it up, finding that extra measure, pushing and pulling. Ecstasy was what he was after, a place to escape to. He would fit himself to the drag and close his eyes. And as he did, here came Rusting, the huge bull bulk of him, the laconic manner of his bearing. The nonchalance with which, to the charges put to him, he quietly responded, 'I didn't do it.' 'Guilty or not guilty, Mr Rusting,' the judge had demanded, and Rusting, looking

6

away, looking at him, *at Fechner*, smiling almost, winking, whispering, 'Not guilty then obviously.' For all his faults, thought Fechner, Rusting had at least the virtue of gall. He would not *cower*.

Edward Fechner, James's father, built ships for thirty years but never sailed in one. He had turned the shame of this into pride, bitter and valuable. He had retired from Harland & Wolff early after a girder caught him sideways, knocking him flat on his back and leaving him with a four-inch scar across his temple. It was a miracle, they said, that he wasn't killed, though Edward didn't believe in miracles. He caught a tidy pension on the back of the accident, which happened as the shipyard was slowly declining anyway, and would occupy himself fixing up cars and motorbikes that he picked up in auctions around the country. Before his mother died, Fechner and his father had had little enough to say to one another. They had nothing at all to say after. They moved around like magnets, positive to positive or negative to negative, refusing connection. Something simmered between them, but it was never named, and in the absence of words it went underground.

At fifteen years old, Fechner was bright enough but had limited application. His teachers, he suspected, enjoyed the fact that he barely existed for them, carrying out his work with unspectacular consistency. He gave them cause neither to praise nor upbraid him. There were though one or two who pushed him harder, referenced an ability he kept dormant. One teacher in particular, a Miss Gower, who taught him biology, had his measure in a way that unnerved him. He was fascinated by the subject: the inner workings of life, the valves and pumps and tubes, the coiled machinery of the potential body. It came from Abraham, of course, he

7

knew, but there was another part, a deeper part, that fascinated him beyond his own understanding. He couldn't help it. And it seemed as though, despite the front he presented, the teenage role he played, Gower could tell. She looked at him sometimes, he felt, as though she could see something in him, inside him, some desire he could not himself even be sure of. And more: she encouraged it. *Yes*, she seemed to be saying. *Yes, James. Go on. Give in.*

So he did.

A murder case has an internal logic, a natural form. It intrigued Fechner to watch it unfold, like a boxing match: jab, feint, counter jab. Though surprisingly placid, mannered. That a crime of passion should be so dispassionately examined – it seemed to Fechner almost obscene, as though the form somehow failed the content. A victory for democracy, for civilisation, no doubt, but he wondered how they'd have done this ten thousand years ago, out of caves. More brutal perhaps, but maybe more honest too.

Fechner's attention moved in waves, like a radio being tuned in and out; grabbing snatches of argument: an assertion here, a counterclaim there. But against Rusting his concentration foundered. As Fechner watched him, Rusting seemed to absorb the space into himself, to destabilise the whole room. The witnesses in this early stretch were largely technical and Rusting would often stare at them with a quizzical, morbid gravity, leaning in as though to check he'd heard them right. There were other times though when he looked bored, above it all, when he had to rub his eyes just to remain present. He hardly ever looked at the jury, and when he did Fechner found himself, for reasons inexplicable, looking down or lifting his hand to his face, as though not to be seen.

The crux of the case was clear by the end of the first

week. Someone – someone almost certainly known to the victim – accosted William Rusting on his way home from the Mermaid Sports & Social Club on Friday night after his performance, strangled him and left him dead some hours later beside the Connswater.

There had been an argument earlier in the evening between William and his son. Rusting had turned up at his father's house at half past five, and ten minutes later – according to at least three eyewitnesses – he left, shouting multiple obscenities. William was a former paramilitary turned community leader, who had spent a significant portion of his son's life in prison. This was not the first clash between them, their animosity well documented. The prosecution was hammering this vitriol home, but Ingram seemed unperturbed, content to accept it, even encourage it. And thereby remove the sting. As an argument Fechner felt it lose its purchase day by day. So Rusting hated his father. Who doesn't?

The jury was divided. A third of them simmered openly at Rusting, baited by his arrogance. Fechner felt them itching to convict, to exercise their unfamiliar measure of power. A couple were ambivalent, suspicious of Rusting but unimpressed with the case being presented against him. One of them, a woman schoolteacher in her late fifties, would tut her way through lunchtimes, convinced she could have made a stronger case herself. 'The incompetence,' she would say, shaking her head. 'Can you believe it?' Fechner watched them all avidly, silently. When asked, he demurred, shrugged in magnanimous hesitation.

At home his wife asked him how it was going.

'I'm not really sure,' he said. 'I mean it's early days.'

'You must already have a sense of whether he did it though?' she asked.

'You're not supposed to pre-judge, Katherine.'

9

'Oh are you not now?' She threw her eyebrows up in mock deference.

Fechner smiled. 'I only mean I'm keeping an open mind.'

'It's like I'm watching a colour version of *Twelve Angry Men*.' Katherine was a doctor too, and also worked at the Royal, albeit in a different department. 'Isn't he an ogre?' she said.

'Who?'

'The accused, whatshisname.'

'Robert Rusting.'

'Rusting, yes. God. Isn't he a Loyalist?' When Katherine said Loyalist it sounded sceptical, like she could hardly believe they existed.

'You remember that's where I'm from,' Fechner said.

'What, Loyalistville?'

'I grew up only a few streets away from where he lives.'

'Loyalisttown.'

Fechner laughed.

'James you are no Loyalist.'

'No,' said Fechner.

'Well, it is heartening to see a man so committed to his constitutional duty that he won't entertain his wife by predicting whether Mr Rusting is guilty. Let me ask it this way then. Would you like to get on the wrong side of Mr Rusting?'

'You know me,' Fechner said. 'I don't like to get on the wrong side of anyone.'

Fechner left school with straight As. Two and a half years of commitment, of dedication. He found, with some surprise, that it was easier to give in to his ability than resist it. The grades just came to him then. Gower beamed her satisfaction. It wasn't until he was sitting with the application forms

10

in front of him that he allowed himself even to consider it: medicine. The province of the wealthy, the perpetual bourgeoisie. It was just about the only profession left that still had the gates up. God knows, anyone could be an accountant now. And lawyers, where would you even start? But a doctor: a doctor was mahogany, Malone Road, the Queen's English. Where would he fit?

Still, he wanted it. The urge had crept up on him, almost unnoticed, a silent tap on his shoulder every few days. He showed the form to his father when he had it completed. His father, sitting in his armchair in front of the TV. 'What's this?' he said. 'University application,' Fechner replied. His father scanned it, found the offending part, looked up at him. 'Really?' he said. 'If I get the grades, obviously,' Fechner responded, cautious. 'Do you think I have money?' his father said, and Fechner said, 'I'll get a loan.' Edward handed him back the form. 'You do whatever you want.'

His whole life, Fechner could never understand just what he had done to annoy his father. Still, even while very young, he sensed in himself a sort of betrayal. As if every piece of interest he parcelled out elsewhere – to his mother, his friends, to Abraham – insulted Edward. Fechner tried to balance his affection, to show his father that it was not a competition, but to no avail. Worse – Fechner knew it *was* a competition, and knew his father knew this. And so, this dividing of love – both Fechner's and his father's – was played out silently, with subtle but determined force. The irony, which Fechner began to realise even at nine or ten years old, was that this knowledge bound them to each other. Their refusal of love, or in his father's case his refusal to accept the division of love, the portion that Fechner could offer him, was itself a form of relationship, stronger in some horrific way than the others.

11

Fechner got the grades and started at Queen's. It was the late eighties. The Troubles simmered, refusing the few frail attempts at resolution. Unionists and Loyalists, buoyed by Paisley, sucked hard on their country. The IRA gave them plenty to work with. The whole thing was vaguely hopeless, but you went on anyway, for want of alternatives. And normal life still functioned, as normal life does, even with helicopters growling overhead.

During the first week of term, Fechner found a room advertised on a noticeboard in the students' union. His flatmates were two boys up from Tyrone, Cormac and Liam, farmers' kids studying agriculture. They wore GAA tops like status symbols, and drank so fast they'd order two pints at once, a lager to keep going while the Guinness settled. He found it exotic how exotic they found Belfast. And they were *Catholic*. Fechner had never cared much himself for the sectarian pull, the colour by numbers. His father was a Protestant, and Unionist by disposition, but peaceable enough. There were few Catholics in his circles. He was not a bigot, he merely fell into the kind of company that came most easily. He went to the parades as a social nicety, not as a fanatic. His mother, by contrast, had hated the whole thing. She refused the Twelfth, but spat venom too at Adams as he mealy-mouthed his apologies on television. Fechner empathised, inasmuch as he could, but her anger was not shareable, and so he found himself outside even that.

Now his life suddenly appeared to him open, untethered. Cormac and Liam were friendly enough, would invite him to join them for the pub quiz in the Eglantine, or to the disco at Hunters, but for the most part they allowed him to do his own thing. He worked hard, much harder than his fellow students, who seemed to him to be completely oblivious to the kind of doubt he found himself relentlessly *in*.

Some of them struggled academically, and he was even able to help them on occasion, with essays, lecture notes and so on. But they had an air of authority that he could never get hold of, a kind of implicit, accepted claim that however difficult they found it, ultimately they were in the right place.

He dated a few girls, girls equally drawn to and perplexed by his manner, his wryness. He was like a student of two, three generations previous, too literal in his attempt to educate himself, insufficiently ironic. It wasn't necessarily that Fechner was uninterested in these girls, but his interest had in it a kind of natural limitation, as though he never truly believed they could really give him anything. He felt this limitation to be an asset. Certainly, as a child, his self-sufficiency was vital and encouraged, if not coerced. He was mystified therefore by the ability these girls had to sacrifice themselves, and to require of him too a neediness that they could assuage, placate. It wasn't that he didn't enjoy their company, or the various lengths to which both he and they would go to enjoy one another (sometimes very far), but rather that he never seemed, to them, in the end, sufficiently at their mercy.

He went with one girl, Sonia, for six weeks at the end of his first year. She was a politics student and competitive swimmer, with a vitality and energy that caused his pulse to quicken when she walked toward him. And she genuinely liked him, drawn perhaps to his seriousness, his quiet, unshowy presence. Perhaps, then, when she told him she thought she was falling in love he should have played along, but as it was he found himself tongue-tied, silent, powerless to respond at all. Worse – when she left, upset, he began to wonder how wise she could really be if she could fall so quickly and needlessly for someone she barely knew.

Fechner felt though, in himself, no superiority. When she told him, a week later, that it was over, he was overcome by

13

an irritation he couldn't fathom, an anger that niggled, inched its way through his body and left in him a dull ache that tied him to his bed for three days, tetchy, frustrated. He barely slept, and when he did he had a recurring dream in which he felt his organs like oil, sitting heavy in his belly. A panic seized him as he realised they had been changed into a womb. He would try to cough it up, in his dream, until he woke himself choking, hawking up in real life nothing but empty air.

He was well liked, for the most part. He was inoffensive, serious. And working class, of course. The well-to-do future doctors – sons and daughters of current doctors, many of them – got off on having as a friend an outsider, someone whose accent caught that bit sharper. He refused to feel patronised by this. They were as stuck as he was, just in leafier streets. He was aware that he had chosen to put himself in their company, that there was something here he wanted, even if he didn't know what it was. And this not-knowing kept him open, alert, primed. Each friendship, though limited, was an exchange; he made sure to get as much as they did, even if ultimately the question of what he was *doing* there remained unanswered. They invited him to birthday parties in big houses in south Belfast, or to hotels with real marble in the toilets, where there was champagne on tap and yet no one had more than a few glasses. He found himself enjoying it, bemused and occasionally wrong-footed but rarely bored. There was a temptation, perhaps, he began to sense; a path to a completely different kind of life being held out to him. Still, it was hard to believe all he had to do was reach out and take it; hard to believe that behind the doors nudging themselves open, there wasn't a sudden drop.

The second week of the trial was mired in technicality. The prosecution seemed to have had a rethink, and abandoning

14

their obsession with motive switched to the detail of the strangling, and the extent to which the presence of Robert's DNA on his father's body could be tied to the killing. It was laborious, but Fechner could feel the case shifting, loosening up. Ingram looked, if not flustered exactly, significantly dismayed. Witness after witness was called, each adding a tiny layer to an increasing weight of evidence that Robert had manhandled William. Rusting had already insisted under oath that earlier in the evening there'd been no violence, only harsh words. The courtroom tightened, the hackle for judgement got up, you could feel it. Once or twice Rusting stared at Ingram in a new way, with inquisitive irritation. Fechner remembered a film he'd seen, about a lepidopterist, who would pin her butterflies down while they were still alive and watch them flutter in vain, thrashing the life out of themselves before settling in beautiful, cold composure. That sense of the cruelty of beauty was recalled to him as he watched Rusting not quite squirm, not quite beat his wings in fear. Fechner knew fear all right, knew the measure of it, the quiet imprint it left behind on seats as patients rose to their operations. All the way he tracked it, from the first meeting when he would talk them through what was to come. He was good at recognising the pitch, the way it played within the body, and he was generous – others had remarked – in his capacity for patience, and in the clarity of his explanations. From the beginning he had this skill, surprising even to himself, his words somehow instinctively forming themselves into the right kind of container for the anxiety of the patient. Where his young colleagues would blurt out their own awkwardness, their own hesitation, Fechner had a sense for the patient's unease, and for their comedy; would manage to bring them gently into his confidence. He could see the encroachment of Rusting's fear:

15

the barely perceptible clench in the jaw, the hand holding the seat, the twitch in the shoulder. He wondered if the others could see it too, his fellow jurors, seated around him. He suspected not. There had been little coherence of argument when they had sat together over food or during breaks, when the facts of the case were scattered around like crumbs, and they went rushing after them, picking them up one by one and throwing them at one another.

On a Thursday morning, a fortnight into the trial, young Kevin leaned down over his shoulder before the session began and pointed out a woman in the upper gallery.

'Joanna,' he nodded.

'Who's Joanna?' said Fechner.

'Rusting's wife.'

He hadn't noticed her before. 'Has she been here all along?'

Kevin shook his head. 'First time.'

A bit younger than Rusting was his first guess, early thirties, her hair a simple, tight bob that framed delicate, almost angular, features. As Rusting was led into the courtroom Fechner saw him look up at her, catch her eye. He feigned a wee trip, made her smile. As the proceedings unfolded she was impassive, calm, unflinching, affecting neither boredom nor particular interest. Yet Fechner detected a sort of keen hunger, her passivity all concentrated into a taut screen. He had the irrepressible conviction that she'd go for your throat if she were hungry.

Absurdly, he was dismayed. In the days he had spent there already, he felt he had come to understand Rusting; he had, in some undefined but compelling way, *access*. Sometimes, he had sensed, he knew Rusting better than Rusting knew himself. He had imagined him with his hands around his father's throat, contracting, bringing an end to the beginning, enacting a balance that had been lost. Up to this point Rusting had seemed entirely of himself, above the fray. Fechner's imagination had been sufficient, but then in walks this woman, with claims he has not considered. And she just sits there, unmoved, arrogant, appropriating to herself attention she has not earned. It thrust upon him the unexpectedly pressing question of Rusting's ownership, his possession by her.

At lunchtime Kevin asked him how he felt the trial was going, whether he felt Rusting was guilty. So unnerved was he by Joanna's appearance that he uncharacteristically blurted out, 'Well it doesn't look good, does it?'

In the summer of his first year, Fechner took a job at McAllisters. It was easy work, carrying coffins, and surprisingly satisfying. It was here that he perfected the quiet, self-effacing manner that would later serve him so well as a doctor, attending silently and carefully to the various griefs that each funeral presented. The democracy of death moved him: its contempt for wealth, fame, religion. There was a strange generosity to it, wisdom even. Abraham was dead only five years, and his reputation conferred on Fechner both privilege and expectation. He found an unexpected satisfaction in the ritual, and in the sense that he knew instinctively how it worked. No one had to tell him when to speak and when to stay silent, when to nod, shake a hand, even offer a tissue. He thrilled to his own intuition. He had always seen himself – not without cause – as something of an outsider, and the experience of university had done little to change this. But here he was, at the heart of things, calm and measured and authoritative. If his mother could see him now.

Cormac and Liam had gone back up to the country, so Fechner had the house to himself. In the long evenings, when it was warm enough, he would sit in the back yard and read paperback Grishams and drink cheap wine. Occasionally he would meet friends in the pub, and once or twice he was invited to a barbecue – always called something else, a 'garden party' or a 'soiree' – out in the country at one of the medics' parents' homes. They laughed when he told them where he was working, and he fed them stories he knew they'd like, mishaps and near disasters. They burned the wrong body at one funeral. 'Sure, it was a closed casket, it didn't matter,' he said, and they squealed in affronted delight. How easily impressed they were.

It got hot that July. The long nights, the sky light until eleven, demanded something, compelled their own arousal. At weekends he began to frequent the few bars still busy with students and invariably would bring home some girl, similarly hungry, buzzing off the same need. They would come home with him willingly – more than willingly, no hint of compunction – and give themselves to him in his bed. The cleanness of it – no talk of a relationship, no demand beyond the demand of the moment – thrilled him but also flattened out the edges, made the event somehow prosaic. He no longer had to fear the headaches, nor the pulling under that would come when he broke up with someone; but he no longer had to fear anything, and that itself felt like a loss. More: he began to get a sense that when he was with these girls, their bodies shifting and twisting, beautiful and free and astonishingly open, that the whole thing had a sort of absence to it. They didn't want to be there, he felt; they wanted to be nowhere, and this was just the best route. And then he wondered, *Is it the girls I'm talking about?*

One Saturday night in August, he brought a girl home from the Eglantine. They were both drunk but not too much. They laughed easily with each other, but he could feel her urgency, the directness of her demand. They almost tore at each other's clothes, and he was inside her in seconds. This is it he thought, and waited for it to happen. But it was just the same. She was there and then quickly she wasn't, she was away wherever it was that she wanted to be, at whatever distance she decided, and he was inside her but he may as well have been in Spain, and the rage then, the overwhelmingness of it as he tried to find it, to make her present. When he opened his eyes and saw her shock, her fear, he immediately pulled back, or almost immediately. They stared at each other. 'What are you doing?' she asked him. 'Nothing,' he said. 'Maybe you should go.' She sat, still, breathing silently. 'Please,' he said. 'Just go.'

On the next day of the trial Joanna was absent. *Her duty fulfilled, she has left him to the dogs.* Fechner shook his head, reprimanded himself. The case was stuck, refused perspicuity; each effort at clarity muddied it further. The prosecution's evidence against Rusting was considerable but almost entirely circumstantial. Ingram had been calling his own witnesses for the guts of a week, but he seemed flustered, biting too quickly at objections. Fechner watched Rusting simmer, but was impressed by how his body somehow mitigated, drew the anger within. He recalled a story Abraham told him as a child, about a man who found a treasure hidden in a field. He covered up the treasure, buried it, then went and sold all that he had and bought the field. He remembered the glee he had experienced on hearing the story, imagining the man's satisfaction, fooling them all. They thought he was just buying a stupid field!

At lunchtimes the jurors were increasingly worked up, their frustration evident. Arguments threatened, then quickly dissipated, fell to whispers. They shouldn't even have been discussing it yet, but how could they not? Fechner moved among them, attending to each but offering little himself. He was good at this listening; reverent, cautious. He was careful to dismiss no one, not even the ones he secretly despised. Coy but generous; quick to smile, to show understanding. And of course, a certain authority still played. He was, after all, a doctor.

He had graduated impressively in the end. It turned out that medicine was as much performance as knowledge, and when the realisation of this sank in, by the start of his final year at Queen's, he discovered a remarkable capacity in himself for occupation, for playing a role. I mean, what else was he doing already, he thought, and yet he'd never grasped it, never abandoned himself to the cause. And when he did, it all started singing, all the discordant notes suddenly in key. What did it matter that he didn't know the song?

By the time he'd finished he struck a more confident figure. A weight had been lifted, the threat of exposure that had always hung just out of frame was now gone, expunged. It gave him a freedom he hadn't previously known. He met Katherine that summer, while still flushed with achievement. He was twenty-three – she was almost five years older. A Dubliner too, albeit a Protestant. Frank, one of the southern students in his year, had held a house party over the Twelfth in Dublin, and a crowd of them had gone down, and there she was, strolling around Frank's parents' Georgian mansion like something from Godard. 'Apparently they call *this* pasta,' was the first thing she'd said to him, and however he'd responded – some off-the-cuff witticism his memory had long abandoned – it seemed to crack her up.

She had been something of a star at Trinity, ambitious. Ruthless with men, it was said. Her friends would look at him when they were first together with a hungered, confused curiosity, wondering what he had that wasn't apparent. The men in her circle eyed her with both wariness and longing. Fechner couldn't shake the image of them as supplicants in a mediaeval court, with her as queen. She was the queen of Dublin 4 anyway. She'd already run through lawyers, accountants, boys living out their parents' lives, stepping into the moneyed world that had been prepared for them. They were cruel yes, but their cruelty was merely a by-product; they wanted to punch Daddy and Katherine just happened to be there instead. That was what she told him anyway, a few months in, when it was already clear that something was going on between them that pulled deeper. It made Fechner wonder. 'Are you saying you want me to hit you?' he asked her once. She said no, but she liked that he would if she asked him to.

Would he though? Fechner was alert to his own faculty for cruelty all right. In the time since his summer of love he'd wound himself in, stopped the pickups, the casual fucking. Or not casual, not exactly; therein the complication. Occasionally he still found himself staying later than his friends on a night out, dancing, caught in the headlights of some bright young thing. And he would let it unfold, give over to the flirtation, even the laying on of hands. But at some point – when she went to the bar, or to the toilet, or to speak to her friends – he would slip away, disappear into safety. By the time he met Katherine he hadn't been with anyone in two years, and had found a sort of monastic peace. Or so he thought.

He was stunned then by the intensity with which he wanted her, right from that first moment. There was something needy in her that projected itself as confidence, that everyone else seemed to read as confidence but he sensed as terror. He tasted it when he kissed her, the violence in her mouth, something insatiable and devouring. Fechner was ready for devouring.

The first holiday they took, to Barcelona, for her twenty-eighth birthday. The brightness, the warm air rushing in off the sea, were like nothing he'd ever experienced. His whole life he'd never been on the Continent. He was like a child in his appreciation, soaking it all up, doggedly thrilled. And Katherine flourished in the sun; she walked up Las Ramblas in Isabel Marant and a pair of Topshop flip-flops, and every man wanted to fuck her. Fechner too, yes, but with a sort of protective restraint, which was going to be, he thought at the time anyway, the making of him. He never could get to the bottom of her need, never adequately account for her presence. It was all presence though. She was really there, eyes open, staring at him as he came in her. She held on to him when they made love as though he might get up at any moment and walk off. It was satisfying all right, what he'd wanted all along, or thought he'd wanted. But it unnerved him too, the way she chose him: he felt she saw something in him, something she had decided to make her own. So he asked her to marry him.

What was it she saw though? He was obsessed, haunted by the idea that there was something *in him*, some secret part – secret even to himself – that other people could see, and he experienced this as a weakness, or a threat, and was unsure how to steel himself against it. And then along came Katherine, all teeth and appetite, stalking something, and when she came to Fechner, rather than look away she dove right in. She never put words to it, and neither did he. Still, their inability to describe to one another what they were each after, and what they were each hiding, coupled with the suspicion that it might be the very thing they each needed; well, who wouldn't build a life around that?

The end of the trial arrived with a sputter. No sudden revelations, no new knowledge, it just juddered to a halt, as though out of steam. The evidence had accreted, slowly but surely, and hung in the air with ominous gravity but without the spectacular display that the drama of the case surely deserved. The judge announced that the following day would see the closing arguments, after which time it would be in the hands of the jury. He sent them home with an admonition to sleep well in anticipation of their forthcoming duty.

On the final morning the summaries were presented; claims rehearsed, restated. A little of the energy that had been present at the beginning returned, as the promise and threat of a verdict approached. Ingram bristled. But he could get no read at all on Rusting himself, sitting transfixed, staring ahead, evacuated. To Fechner he was like a yogi, a guru, exercising his detachment. But the case angled heavy against him, and Ingram's disquiet appeared only to affirm what was coming.

In closing, the judge reminded the jury members of their responsibility. 'A man's future is in your hands,' he said. 'Be circumspect, thoughtful, careful in your deliberations. Weigh the evidence thoroughly. Do not be afraid to ask questions of one another. Be open to what each of you has to say.' As they were led out of the court Fechner spotted Rusting with his head lowered, conferring with Ingram. Ingram, anxious still, whispered something, but Rusting set his hand gently on his knee, shook his head and smiled.

The deliberation room was as clichéd as he'd imagined it; a long table surrounded by twelve chairs, the walls insistently blank. The first task was to elect a foreman.

'Foreperson,' said Vicky, a marketing manager in her thirties.

Kevin bit back. 'It doesn't have to be a man, that's not what I meant.'

'Language is important,' Vicky said.

It went back and forth like this for a while, snappy, fractious. The muted environment of the courtroom, in which they had to sit in silence and bite their tongues, gave way to the appetite to argue, to present themselves. Eventually someone asked for a volunteer, and Vicky shot her hand up. Fechner's heart leapt with unwilled excitement. After a brief silence she said, 'Well if there's no one else.'

'I wonder,' said Kevin, 'if we shouldn't propose someone. Like, not ourselves.'

Fechner ached in gratitude. He knew Kevin hated Vicky, had expressed this hostility both directly and indirectly. But his timing, his glorious timing! It was astonishing to see it all so vividly, so precisely. Vicky biting back her rage. 'Well, somebody has to do it. We can't sit here all day.'

'If I might,' Fechner said, quietly. 'Perhaps before we make that decision, we should take a survey of how we all feel about the case. How we would vote now, if we had to.' A few heads nodded, the room shifting towards agreement, as he knew it would. But he waited for Vicky.

'Yes,' she said, eventually. 'All right.'

'First, the guilty,' Fechner said. A softness had been introduced, a humour, that he felt the group rise to, appreciate. Six of the twelve raised their hands, Vicky among them.

'And the not guilty?' Two hands went up, tentative.

Fechner turned to the three remaining, Kevin one of them. 'And you, like me, are undecided? Well, it seems like we do have some work to do,' Fechner said.

24

One of the elders of the group, a retired bookkeeper in her sixties, suggested that perhaps one of the undecideds should be chairperson. The three others quickly declined and Fechner was left as the only runner.

'Unless there are any objections?' he said, watching Vicky's hands go under her legs, the tiny, silent shake of her head. The image came to him, for one startling moment, of his mother in her bed, her halted, ineffectual movements, gestures collapsing halfway through. He blinked the memory away. 'Well,' he said. 'Then my first action will be to propose they bring us coffee.'

For the rest of the day they argued and debated and quarrelled. Fechner was careful to let everyone speak, let each opinion be heard. At times this brought a calmness, his own manner – studious, conciliatory – acting as a boundary that kept the conversation peaceable. But at moments their appetite for argument – the animal need to have their own voice recognised – threatened to burst out, to run wild. In particular, a young entrepreneur called Josh, who had what Kevin had earlier described to Fechner as a punchable face, trilled to his own convictions. He was joined ably by Vicky – the pair of them shaking their heads and tutting and raising their voices, talking over the hesitations of the others. For them, there was no doubt whatsoever that Rusting was guilty, and their arguments, as the day progressed, dominated.

Fechner had never felt so alive. In surgery the patient is, to all measures, inert; the only test the precision of his own skill. But here the challenge was continuously moving, a writhing, belligerent hydra, a monster that could be defeated not merely by skill but by cunning. He sensed himself rise to it, reckon and measure and adjust, stalk the beast. He felt – irony not lost – like Rusting himself, hammering the world into the

25

shape it should be, simplifying. Purifying. Fechner felt the man he really was, or was meant to be, hidden for years, was breathing, calling, growing within him.

At one point, Josh was speaking, almost shouting. His indignation sang, his disbelief at the sheer foolishness of his fellow jurors. Fechner felt the shift already, those originally convinced of Rusting's guilt beginning to prevaricate, dissociate. He poked a little, gently, and in came Vicky, her certainty bared.

'I don't understand,' she said, 'how we're even still debating this. It's so obvious.'

It was the *obvious*, he thought, that tipped them. The flinch in the shoulders, all the others inching back, beginning to distance themselves. He knew he must wait for his moment, must be careful not to move too soon, but god the excitement, the kick.

'I wonder,' he said, 'if it might be worth us once again having a show of hands? We've all had a chance to impress upon one another our convictions. Just to see where we are now in relation to this morning?'

They agreed.

'I suppose,' Fechner continued, 'the one thing to remember is that – and this might be easier for us now than it was this morning – we're not voting on whether we *think* Rusting is guilty but whether we are *certain* he is guilty.' He felt the sweat bead inside his collar. It was so innocuous, this gentle pressure he applied, a feather on the back of an elephant. But it felt to him like an anvil.

'Okay,' he said. 'The guilty.'

There was a beautiful hesitation. Even Josh and Vicky paused before sticking their hands up. Tentatively, a couple of other hands also rose.

'And the not guilty?'

26

Six hands went up, all but Kevin's. Fechner gently lifted his own hand and then set it back down.

'Well,' he said, 'on we go.'

And they went on, but the turn had happened, the damage was done. At the close of the day, Fechner was called in to the judge to report on where the jury were with their decision. Fechner sensed his approval; the judge grateful that he was dealing with a fellow professional. Fechner told him that they were making progress but could not be certain of a unanimous verdict.

'A unanimous verdict is always best,' the judge said.

Fechner nodded, sober.

'You are sure?'

'I try to stop people dying of cancer,' Fechner said. 'Who among us can be sure of anything?'

The judge smiled, weary. 'If I permit a majority of ten, would that allow you to reach a decision?'

Fechner ensured the surge of joy went unnoticed. 'I think it might, yes.'

'I'd prefer not to run this trial again,' the judge said. Fechner felt him stiffen, fall back into his authority. 'Ten jurors I'll accept.'

Fechner's regret was that he did not see it for himself. He watched later, at home, on television; Rusting's smile disarming in its frank openness. Relief, surely, but also glee, even mockery. Fechner's wife Katherine was surprised by what Rusting looked like. Not thuggish, as she'd assumed. 'Artless' was how she described him. Fechner showed her on a laptop, scrolling back and forth, playing and replaying the scene on the steps outside the courtroom, Ingram proclaiming his platitudes about justice while beside him Rusting stood silent, ratifying in his blunt, free body his own innocence.

The following morning, Fechner woke to the sound of the radio downstairs, Katherine busying herself in the kitchen. The wine from last night had him fuzzy, unwilling. He lay there a moment, letting it dissipate. When he heard the front door shut, he grabbed the laptop and found that the thrill was not diminished, even as it receded. He felt it acutely, painfully almost,· the sense that time was already inserting itself, distancing him from the last few weeks, correcting. It struck him as unjust that he should have played such a role and yet gone unnoticed. Unappreciated. There was no other way it could be, he knew. But it had started already to leave a taste in his mouth, ashy, bitter. There he is again, Rusting, shoulders out, indifferent to the architect of his success. Worse – the thought darted through Fechner's mind unbidden, before he could prevent it – Rusting's credulity, thinking it was Ingram who saved him, Ingram who performed the miracle. Ingram! Standing there, bristling with importance, taking questions like treats. *A dog, a little lapdog, that's all he is.*

But he knew this would not do, Fechner. Beauty is its own reward. He zoomed in, two fingers, as Rusting spoke his only lines: 'I'd like to thank everyone who believed in me. You will not be forgotten.'

2

Summer rolled round, and all of a sudden it was roasting, Belfast soaking in its own juices. It's always like this: joy descends, everyone astounded again that such heat is possible. From his office, high up in the hospital tower, Fechner watched the city lying on its back below, spread out for his attention. Lunchtimes he tended to spend on his own, drinking coffee from a flask, eating something one of the nurses had fetched for him, imagining the street life teeming. Teeming perhaps a stretch, for Belfast.

On days like these he could see the distant shimmer, the heat and light combine to sublimate buildings, turn the bricks liquid. The whole city felt like a mirage. The trial by now was history, just another footnote in a city cluttered with them. In the intervening months, life had regained its safe mundanity. Fechner worked through his list of patients. There were those he warmed to more than others, whose cases he would have liked to attend more closely. But usually it was just a post-diagnosis consultation, a follow-up to plan surgery, and then they were simply machines for repair, laid out before him, faulty parts exposed. He could not even, at this stage, feel their need, their hunger. Though on occasion, mid-operation, he would sense some palpable force emerging not from their consciousness but from the body itself, some voracious will or desire seeking assertion, desperate for recognition. There was no telling in which patients this would arise; once, with a woman in her nineties who was so frail they almost didn't operate, he was seized by such a violent insistence that he stepped back, nearly knocking over an attendant. He did his job, sewed her up and she lived for years still. For the most part though he carried out his task in mute competence, no drama, no sentiment. It seemed to him, more than ever since the trial, absurd that his job should be so *inhuman*. He wasn't sure if the dissatisfaction this brought had been heightened, but it sat on his shoulder now like a tiny, silent, insistent bird, watching his movements, refusing to comment, catching his eye and then turning away.

For a change he decided to go out for lunch. He had a bowl of ramen at one of the new places the students frequented. As he walked back, he noticed a young man just thirty yards ahead of him grab the arm of a woman. At first Fechner thought they knew each other, that the man was simply getting her attention, but as he came closer, he realised that the woman was frightened, staring blindly at the man. 'Hey,' Fechner tried to shout, but it came out feeble, barely audible. He was practically on them now. He mumbled a few phrases, attempts. The man turned to him. Not a man really, a boy, sixteen or seventeen, Fechner realised, flat faced, skinny, high. 'Fuck you right off,' he said. Fechner felt a rage, a pulsing, live anger run through him, but he just stood there, transfixed, mute. The woman pleaded, 'Do something', but he was powerless, his own body on the cold metal table, exposed, frozen. The boy snatched the woman's bag, yanked it from her arm. When she reached out for it, he shoved her and she toppled backwards, landing hard on the pavement. The boy took off in a sprint down Sandy Row. A car pulled up, and a young woman climbed out and helped the victim to her feet. Fechner was all attention then: 'Are you okay, are you hurt?' She stared at him, fear giving way to disgust. She started dusting herself down, straightening her clothes. 'Can you call the police for me?' she asked the girl. Fechner stood there, dumb. Eventually she turned to him. 'You can go,' she said, nodding her head down the street, flicking her hand dismissively. As though she knew where he was going. As though she knew everything there was to know about him.

For Katherine's birthday at the end of September Fechner booked a table at a new Italian restaurant on the Malone Road.

'To you,' Fechner raised his Nero d'Avola. Katherine clinked his glass with hers.

'Do you still find me attractive, James?'

'Well, of course I do,' said Fechner.

'We haven't done this in a while,' she said.

The waiter brought their mains. For Katherine, roasted cauliflower with fennel, black olives and toasted almonds. Fechner had sea bream with chicory and garlic.

'How is it?' she said, a few bites in.

'Yes, it's fine,' said Fechner. He was nibbling slowly, pushing the food around.

'You've barely touched your fish.'

He shrugged.

'What's wrong with it?'

'Nothing. It's just. It's maybe a little underdone.'

Katherine reached across, speared a piece, put it in her mouth.

'My God,' she said, spitting it out. 'Call the waiter over.'

31

'No, it's all right,' said Fechner.

'It's not all right, what are you talking about? It's practically still swimming.'

'I've left it too long, don't worry about it. I'm not that hungry anyway.'

'Oh for God's sake James,' she said. She raised a hand in the air. The waiter came quickly across.

'My husband's fish is not cooked. Take it away and replace it please.'

'Oh, I'm sorry madam,' he said. He looked at Fechner, the slightest hint of a smirk on his face. 'Let me take that sir, shall I.'

They both watched him into the kitchen.

'You can carry on,' Fechner said.

Katherine sighed.

A few minutes later the waiter returned with a new fish, freshly prepared. He set it in front of Fechner. 'The chef sends his sincere apologies.' With exaggerated deliberateness he turned to Katherine. 'If there's anything else you need help with just let me know.'

'What is it you think you owe them?' Katherine said when the waiter had left.

'Owe who?'

She shook her head.

'You're in your forties now, James.'

'What does that mean?'

'You tell me,' she said. 'You tell me.' She collected herself. 'Let's just have a nice evening shall we.'

On the Saturday before Christmas, Fechner knocked on his father's door. The day was freezing, and he stood there in the damp air, listening to the pigeons murmur and coo, flap their ratty wings. Fechner's father was pushing eighty. He lived alone, apart from his birds, in a tiny red-brick terrace down near Victoria Park. The house was barely furnished, like a hostel for someone leaving prison.

His father opened the door.

'It's you,' he said.

'Yes,' said Fechner.

'I'm going out soon,' said Edward.

'I'll not stay long.'

'All right.' Edward turned and walked into the house.

From the pocket of his overcoat Fechner pulled out a gift. He handed it to his father.

'What's this for?'

'It's just a little Christmas present.'

'Right. I don't have anything for you.'

'Well, it doesn't matter,' said Fechner.

Edward unwrapped a notebook, and a beautiful vintage fountain pen, deep opalescent burgundy and black.

'It's a Conway Stewart 58,' Fechner said. 'Gold nib. Made in the thirties.'

'Yes,' his father stared at it. 'Am I supposed to write my memoirs or something?'

The noise from the birds in the back yard was getting louder. Edward set down the pen and notebook and walked out to them. The pigeons were housed in a wooden loft attached to the rear of the house, jutting out above the bare, flagged yard. When he'd built it, twenty years before, the neighbours complained, but he ignored them. Fechner had briefly tried to intervene, in vain. Eventually the woman and her daughter moved away.

He watched his father empty seed into plastic bowls and place them into the coop, the birds squabbling immediately around each. Then he picked the birds up, one by one, held them, stroked them.

'There, there, Marcus; there, there, Tonto,' he said. He ran his fingers along one bird's back, over its crown, delicate. He picked up a handful of seeds and let it peck right out of his open hand.

He held out one of the birds to Fechner. 'Here, take him,' he said.

'No, it's all right.'

'I need to get something from the house.'

Fechner shook his head.

'Just take the fucking bird,' his father said and shoved it into his hands.

Fechner stood there holding it, feeling it pulse and hustle. He could sense the heat in its blood. He stood there in silence, shivering with cold and disgust. He closed his eyes but the bird persisted, wriggling away with its vivid carnal life. When he looked again, he saw his father watching from the kitchen. He came out, took the bird off Fechner, gently ran a finger over its head, his scooped hand filled still with seeds.

'What's wrong with you?' he said.

Fechner said nothing.

The doctors from all of the Belfast hospitals got together every year for an annual Christmas do. On this occasion it was in the golf club at Malone, on the day before Christmas Eve. It was organised by a colleague of Fechner's, Robert Murphy. Murphy was an eye surgeon – a looker, he called himself, with insistent humour. Fechner liked him all right, albeit from a distance. More a colleague than a friend. He was a big lad, Murphy; tall, heavyset, exaggerated swagger. He had played rugby when he was younger, and you could tell: that half-fat half-muscle aspect, hands like shovels. He was something of a character and liked to play up to it, so he decided to give the party a theme: Gatsby.

Murphy was popular, so they all bought in, found outfits online and showed up like West Egg regulars, gowns and tuxes and hair plastered flat with Brylcreem. As they arrived, students playing waiters served them highballs. Katherine wore a beige silk dress with sequins, cut at the knee, straight off Carey Mulligan. Fechner was surprised how much she'd gone all out – not only the dress but the silver tiara, the elbow-length silk gloves, the earrings like sleek, glittering pyramids. She'd had her hair done the day before, her normal shoulder-length style chopped to a bright, weightless bob. She shimmered as they walked in. He saw the eyes drawn to her, watched her embrace their attention, rise to it.

'Well, look at you,' Murphy said when he saw her. 'Beautiful.'

She smiled and clinked her glass with his.

'James,' he said to Fechner. 'You look ... tremendous. Perhaps more socialist than socialite though.'

Katherine laughed.

Fechner's closest friend at work – his only friend, one might not unfairly say – was an older gentleman in his early sixties called Charles Buchanan. Like Fechner, Buchanan was also a surgeon, with a reputation as something of an artist. No one wielded a knife quite like Buchanan, people said, though Buchanan was quite undisturbed by such fame. He was almost pathologically unshowy. Wry, dour, percep- tive, with a sense of humour drier than sandpaper, he came from money but didn't quite fit the picture, which Fechner appreciated. Dinner was over, and a student band, dressed for the occasion, was murdering a farrago of ragtime and jazz. Fechner and Buchanan sat in the corner nursing beers, watching the dancing. It was special, a little moment: thirty or forty of them shaking and jiving, the lights catching mil- lions of sequins in an endless flash.

'Your wife,' Buchanan said, 'seems born to this.'

Fechner stared at Katherine, dancing with Murphy. Some knowledge stirred in him, though it wasn't knowledge, it couldn't be knowledge. It *felt* like knowledge though. She shook her head, her hair bouncing, lifting from side to side; her hands in agreement in front of her, swinging long loops. *No no no*, they were saying. *Yes yes yes*. When the band finished one of its pieces, Murphy leaned in and kissed Katherine on the cheek. It would have been nothing really, nothing at all, were it not for the furtive, animal glance she turned on the room afterwards.

He'd never done anything like it before. They were just in the door, a little after one in the morning. The wine from the party sung through Fechner's blood, but he wouldn't blame that. Katherine was removing her make-up in the bathroom. First he checked her jacket pockets: empty. And then her clutch. Among the usual items he fixed on a small, black jewellery box, velvet. He opened it. Inside, an opal teardrop pendant he'd never seen before. And a card: 'To Daisy, from Jay x.'

The thought of confrontation is both enlivening and terrifying. He pictures himself, bold, authoritative, presenting to Katherine her obligations and failures, asking her just what she thinks she is doing. But he doesn't convince. He is struck that the sense of betrayal he feels is balanced by a feeling of rightness, that Katherine is surely justified in turning her attention elsewhere. If anything, it is little short of miraculous that it has taken her so long. And the strange, sickly satisfaction of having his own weakness affirmed. This is all he really deserves, is it not? Such a poor little breast to latch on to, but he sucks at it anyway.

3

A couple of months later, a friend of Buchanan's died, some-body he'd known since university. Fechner didn't know him well but had met him a few times, played cards with him, shared a pint in company. It was sudden, a stroke, out of nowhere; Buchanan was shaken up. Fechner felt for his friend. The funeral was out of Brown's Funeral Directors in east Belfast, not half a mile from where Fechner had grown up. It was a bitter, wet March day, the air filled with needles. A regular enough sight on the Newtownards Road too: a group of thirty or so, mostly elderly and middle-aged men, huddled outside on the pavement after the service, murmuring against the cold through thick scarves, awaiting the hearse.

Finally, it rolled out, crawled down the road towards Dee Street. Fechner had not planned on staying for this part but found himself drawn along, unwilling to leave Buchanan alone. As the contingent neared the turn-off where they would disband and leave the body to its journey alone Fechner spotted him, standing outside the White Star Line pub: Robert Rusting. He was barely thirty feet away, staring indifferently at the hearse as it crept past.

It was more than a year since the trial, but he seemed,

to Fechner's eyes, exactly the same, pure self-containment, needless. It struck Fechner that he had never seen him outside the courtroom. It was a surprising thrill, a sort of amplification. His mouth dried up. He felt his footsteps heavy, thudding, like he'd forgotten how to walk. Buchanan gave him a look.

When the hearse finally accelerated off, the mourners did the handshakes, the regular chatter, the shared relief that at least it hadn't been them. Life's guileless persistence.

'Are you going to the house?' Fechner asked Buchanan.

He shook his head.

Fechner nodded to the bar. 'Will we take in a pint then?'

He could hardly believe himself. He pulled his hat down and his scarf up. He felt his heart large, exquisite. The White Star Line was busy enough for a weekday afternoon. Along the front, below the street windows, all of the tables were occupied. The bar was straight ahead, and the left-hand wall was hugged by a red leatherette bench and a few more tables. There was no smoking, but Fechner felt the air cloying, thick. The windows were tinted, the light that made it through murky, anaemic. Buchanan nodded Fechner towards an unoccupied table right at the back while he went to the bar.

Fechner settled himself against the banquette, looked around as discreetly as possible. He took it all in: the sticky floor, the *Titanic*-themed paraphernalia, the wall of faded photographs of Ballymacarrett FC squads from the fifties. A fruit machine in the corner blushed and jingled. He kept his hat on, his scarf up. He could see more or less the entire room from where he was, but there was no Rusting. He wondered briefly if he'd conjured him up. And then suddenly he burst into view, emerging from a side door Fechner had overlooked. He sat down at one of the tables at the front, his back to Fechner, opposite a couple of men, one older and one younger. The pair of them sat there staring at Rusting, eager, anticipatory, deferential. Finally Rusting shook his head and they moved back in their seats, disappointed. A failed bet, wondered Fechner. Or marriage.

Fechner and Buchanan sipped away on their pints, toasting the latter's lost friend. Buchanan was sentimental, emotional. Fechner kept glancing away towards the front of the bar. He felt Buchanan become agitated, and was relieved to get up for a round. He shuffled to the bar, rearranging his scarf, pulling it tighter and higher, Lawrence of Arabia. He was five feet off Rusting now, could reach out and touch him if he wanted. He made his order.

'You were at the funeral?' the barman said.

'What?' said Fechner.

'The funeral.' He nodded towards the road.

'Yes,' said Fechner.

'I'm sorry for your loss.'

'Thank you,' he mumbled.

He could hear Rusting's voice but couldn't quite make out what he was saying. He stood there, shivering with proximity. And then, without warning, Rusting was beside him. The smell of cologne, tart and sweet, was a surprise. He was still a couple of feet away, but Fechner felt as though he'd been jostled aside. Rusting ordered his round and returned to his seat without a glance. Fechner could feel every molecule of the sticky wood of the bar answer his fingers.

He returned to his seat with the pints.

'Are you all right?' Buchanan said.

'Of course I'm all right,' Fechner said. 'I mean, I'm okay. What kind of a day is this? How are you supposed to feel?'

They sipped their pints to completion in companiable silence. Buchanan declined Fechner's offer of another. They gathered themselves, buttoned up against the weather. As they left Fechner kept his head down. Buchanan had booked a taxi on his phone.

'You sure you don't want a lift?' he said.

'I appreciate it, Charles. It's okay, I've a few things to do this side.'

Fechner watched the taxi off then took his bearings. Other than visiting his father he hadn't been in this part of the city in years. The bingo hall still stood forlorn, a run-down pebble-dash building with two fat ladies hand-painted above an incongruous frosted glass entrance, like a misplaced dentist's. Fechner watched an old woman come out, wrap her plastic mac tight against the cold, shake her head. He felt alive, alert to everything, everyone. He watched her set off up the back street towards the Albertbridge Road, hauling her shopping cart behind her like a resistant animal. He was filled with useless, overwhelming sympathy. Just past the bingo hall and across the street was Beatties chippie. He'd give it an hour, he told himself. He ordered a fish supper and found a seat by the window with a view across to the bar.

He hadn't eaten fish and chips in years – Katherine wouldn't stoop so low – and he was surprised by how much he enjoyed it. He remembered Friday evenings with Abraham, if they'd been working together, calling in at the Hot Spot on the way home for cod and pasties. *Don't tell your father.* And he didn't, but still his father must have known. 'Do you know that fish are one of the filthiest creatures?' his father had announced one night, as Fechner stepped through the door late, and then turned back to the television.

He watched the White Star Line. Punters came and went, but no one he recognised. He dragged out the chips, made them last as long as he could, but he finished and there was still no Rusting. It was a sign. He should know better.

He was wrapping up again when out Rusting stepped, on his own, squeezing himself into a big black puffa. Fechner recalled the impression he'd had during the trial, of time collapsing, Rusting's adult bravado giving way to his boyishness, his youth. Rusting closed his eyes and seemed to sniff the air, as though catching a scent, a trail. He set off then, away from Fechner, up the Newtownards Road.

Fechner followed. Fifty yards. A group of young ones traipsed past, giddy with drink. Rusting nodded at them, and they nodded back. Plenty of people on the street; Fechner was not unduly conspicuous. And yet how the heart pounded, the pricked skin tingled. At the junction, Rusting crossed, Fechner behind, catching up now, too excited for his own good. They went through the car park, caught the Connswater Path and followed it up to Beersbridge. Just before the main road, Rusting stopped, sudden. Fechner froze. He was out in the open now, no tree or building or God to hide him. He willed him to keep moving, but Rusting just stood there, assessing the wind, thrown. Then he half-turned and without looking back towards Fechner broke off for one of the side streets.

A squeal from the playground below shucked Fechner back to life. He reached the street just as Rusting rounded the corner. It was a risk, but he felt, after all this, touched. Something was on his side. He walked quickly now, almost ran. But this was it, this was the real. Sell everything, buy the fucking field. At the corner he pulled up, peered cautiously around. And God poured his blessings down upon him. There was Rusting, pushing through a little green gate, fumbling briefly with his key before fronting the door and disappearing.

Abraham once told Fechner that a man's life is nothing more than a collection of seconds. The next thirty saw

Fechner dead and reborn a hundred times. His feet don't break stride as he approaches, as he passes, as he turns at the corner into the next street. 'Number sixty-three,' he repeats to himself. 'Number sixty-three. Number sixty-three.'

On the Friday evening that followed, Katherine told him she was going over to her friend Maria's.

'Maria's, eh?' he said.

'Yes, Maria's. I'll probably be late.'

He bit his tongue. If her deception hurt, his own shame stung sharper.

When she left he propped himself in front of the TV with a laptop on his knee. Rusting's Facebook was private, but Fechner still found a handful of photos. He began to connect faces to names, and noted them down in his phone. There were a few images from Orange parades, and a few of Rusting and Joanna in groups at parties. He never seemed lairy, like a lot of the others, draped around one another, hammered. Rusting was somehow above it all, separate, imperious. In one image, from a party Fechner deduced must have been in Rusting's own home, he pours wine into a row of glasses, the wine spilling over the edges, Rusting laughing, his broad face beaming satisfaction, generosity, provision. A crowd watch on, revelling in Rusting's glee, his offering. *A priest*, thought Fechner, not without irony: bounteous, generous to a fault, dispensing his own self as sacrament.

Fechner also dug up a couple of court cases on old news sites – one for unpaid fines, and one for intimidation and intent to cause harm, for which Rusting was convicted and given probation. The conviction was ten years old; he would have been still in his twenties. There was no information about the victim, but Fechner could not but imagine the young lad on Sandy Row, Rusting's hand at his throat, whispering, gently but with clarity and insistence, taking the woman's bag back, disabusing the boy of the paltry claim he had tried to make.

At eleven he stepped into the garden and called Maria.

'Maria, I'm so sorry to be calling this late. Listen, I'm just home and I've lost my keys, I'm locked out, and Katherine's not answering her phone. Can you tell her I'll nip over and get hers?'

Maria's silence shimmered. He could practically hear her running through her options. 'She's just in the bathroom, I'll get her to call you back.'

'No problem, sure I'll order a cab here, shouldn't be long.'

The moon was almost full, only a tiny sliver cut off. The air breathed a hint of warmth, spring threatening, promising. Fechner felt the beautiful violence of new life on the way, the earth ready to start again. Fresh bulbs trembling to be flowers, vibrating already in the damp muck, sucking it all in to give it all out again. Every fucking year, isn't it incredible? If you got to design it yourself would you do it any different, everything in its right place, the dead giving way to the living, which themselves become the dead, the chain of rank, insistent life. If you can't trill to this, what can you trill to? Are you even born?

His hand buzzed and he answered.

Maria's voice shook, hesitant. 'James,' she said, 'it's just, Katherine—'

'Maria, I'm an idiot,' he cut in. 'Would you believe it, the keys were in my pocket all along. Madness. Sorry. Tell Katherine it's all right, everything's sorted, I'm good.'

He dropped his phone into his pocket, looked up at the glassy sky, filled his lungs with air. Caught the scent. Are you even born?

4

April arrived. Evenings lingered, birds horny for summer, singing late and loud. Fechner booked a week off work, told Katherine he was going fishing in Galway. Instead, he rented an Airbnb just off the Albertbridge Road, near the Iron Hall where Abraham once took him, at seven years old, to see the Templemore Hall Male Voice Choir. They were all dead now, but he could still see them every time he walked past, hear their deep, rough, sturdy voices combine, loaded on worship, balanced between harmony and violence. He remembered one of them, a friend of Abraham's, asking him afterwards if he enjoyed it. 'Would you like to be a singer?' he'd said, and when Fechner nodded, the man hit him on the chest. 'It's all in there,' he said, *tap tap tap.*

The first thing he did was get a haircut. He went out of town, a small place he found just by driving around, outside of Lisburn. Fechner's hair was unremarkable, had always been, by his own measure, unremarkable. No shoulder-length teenage rebellion for him. Blandly dark, giving to grey now at the edges, swept to one side by an evident comb. It was a hairstyle from every era and none, and he'd never worn it any other way, not even as a child. The barber's was quiet of a Monday morning, the old boy who ran it working alone.

Fechner told him to shave it off.

'What number?'

Fechner was thrown.

The barber looked him up and down. 'Are you sure?'

'I want a change,' Fechner said, already mollifying, already justifying himself. Once again the quease, the softness.

'Do you mind?' the old boy said, and without waiting for an answer he set his hands on top of Fechner's head. Fechner caught his eye, looked away. He began to move his hands around, assessing. 'You just need to have a certain kind of head to carry it off.' His fingers caressed Fechner's skull. Fechner tried to hold himself steady. 'Well, I think actually yours is perfect. Shall we go number one?'

Fechner kept his eyes closed throughout. When the barber finished, he cracked his eyes, stared back at himself. The close crop drew a line. He felt tighter, sharper.

He bought new clothes too, but he couldn't get them to sit right, too many years noosed into a tie. So he roughed up a few of his older pieces, went into the yard of the rental and rubbed the trousers against the wall. He wasn't sure what he was doing, but it worked. He put them on and he felt different: coarser, unleashed. Somehow, with his hair gone, his eyes had popped out, demanded attention. There was a wild pierce in them he hadn't noticed before, not unattractive.

On Tuesday afternoon, it begins. He steps into the White Star Line. He's wearing navy slacks and a white shirt, pulled about a little, and a fairly classy beige duffel that he picked up in the War on Want on Dee Street.

The bar was quieter than before. The barman who'd served him then was absent, in his place a young woman.

The patrons, five or six of them, were scattered around, mostly alone, sucking their amber. No Rusting. Fechner carried his pint to a table, unfolded his paper. He's not here for this, but it affords some satisfaction anyway, a life he avoided, feared even, and here it is with its own stillness, its own modest boon.

When he finished the first pint, the barmaid brought him another. She introduced herself as Camile.

'That's a lovely name,' Fechner said.

'Aye I know,' she said, and then laughed.

Barely twenties, but her face pleaded older. She went in for kindness, he guessed. Too much kindness, likely. She asked him about himself. A doctor with a week off, he told her. His father was poorly so he'd come to stay with him for a few days. You don't look like a doctor. No, what do I look like? The blush, the headshake. It's a banter Fechner doesn't get in his moneyed world and he likes it. He's enjoying being back in the neighbourhood, yeah. Sure, it never really leaves you does it. She told him she cared for her mother who's in a wheelchair but still managed to create havoc inside and out on a daily basis. She sounds like quite a woman. You can have her if you want.

His humour lifted. By the time he'd finished his second pint he was ready to go. Fechner was never a drinker – never loved the looseness that came with it – and the thin metallic finesse of Carlsberg wore off swift. Just before he got up to leave, however, in the door came a youngster, one of the people he had seen sitting with Rusting. He was agitated, twitchy, rippling his fingers on the bar like a monkey at a piano. Fechner tried not to watch him but failed. The kid was talking to Camile, but she was having none of it. He caught Fechner's eye on him. His legs were shuffling too, spastic. The turmoil practically spilling out of him.

47

'D'you want a photo?' he said.

'Are you all right?' Fechner said.

'Who are you?' The confrontation seemed to substantiate him. The shaking briefly subsided. Fechner's affection deepened.

'You should talk to him,' Camile said, nodding towards Fechner. 'He's a doctor.'

'Is he fuck,' said the boy.

'You seem discomposed,' Fechner said.

'What's that?'

'Agitated. Troubled.'

'What's it to you?'

'Why don't you sit down?'

With his leg Fechner pushed out the chair opposite him. 'A pint for my friend, Camile,' he said.

The boy sat down. He was eyeing Fechner still, wary, but his body had started to obey him, the fidget-fuckery giving way to something, maybe just potential affray. He gripped the edge of the table like he would float off otherwise.

'Are you a pervert or something?'

'I'm James Fechner,' Fechner said. 'What's your name?'

'Polio.'

'Polio?'

'I mean it's Paul, but I get Polio.'

'Why's that?'

Polio sighed like he was ancient. 'It's, like, everything. My health isn't very good like. Are you really a doctor?'

Fechner nodded. Camile appeared, set the pint on the table. Polio looked at Fechner, wary.

'Go ahead,' said Fechner.

The boy lifted the glass, took a long gulp, set it back down. 'What do you fix?' he said.

'What do you have?'

48

Polio laughed again. A bit more torture in it than before, Fechner sensed.

'Who fucken knows.'

'What does your doctor say?'

'He says it's nerves. Like it's all in my head. "Get out of your head, get out of your head," he goes on.' His fingers were away again, all calypso. 'Does this look like nerves to you?'

'What does he give you?'

Polio produced a strip of pills, tiny white dots. 'They do fuck all,' he said. 'Fucken TicTacs.'

'Try something,' Fechner said. 'Put your hands on the table, like this,' Fechner placed his palms flat on the surface, 'and wrap your feet around the chair legs.'

'Wise up.'

'I'm serious,' said Fechner. 'Trust me.'

He stared at Fechner. Fechner held his scepticism. Polio blinked caution, but he set his glass down and did it.

'Now close your eyes.'

'Fuck off.'

'Serious. I'm not going to do anything.'

Polio sucked in, wavered. The torture was back, Fechner felt it, but something else too, some wild, cruel longing. Polio closed his eyes. His face – blanched, skinny, pockmarked, with tiny, rune-like scars below his ears – contorted, with desire and shame.

Fechner noticed Camile watching, intrigued, but he ignored her.

'All right,' he said. 'Feel your hands. Your fingers.'

'What do you mean? I can feel them.'

'No, *feel* them. Feel what they feel like. What's happening in them, what are they doing? What are they saying? Don't try to stop them, or fix them. Just feel them.' Fechner felt the pressure on the table, Polio's knuckles deathly white.

'And your eyes now. Keep them closed, but soften them. Don't fight. Your shoulders too, loosen them. Loosen them, yes, like that.'

And it happened, it really happened. Polio's knuckles coloured, his body visibly, palpably let go. All the jitter, all the coil, unravelled.

'That's it,' Fechner said, and Polio sat there, hands flat, wrapped to the chair, briefly, tantalisingly present. He was silent. Fechner was silent. Camile's mouth gaped O. The other punters were all watching. After maybe thirty seconds, Fechner said, 'All right.'

Slowly, Polio blinked back into the room. His weak, fluey eyes were wet, a tear in the corner of one threatening the top of his cheek. He sat silent, stared at his hands with incomprehension.

Fechner stood up. 'All right well. I have to be going. You take care of yourself son.' He laid a fiver on the bar, threw a nod to Camile as he left. 'I'll see you again,' he said.

The temptation to return was strong, but he resisted. His luck held once, his horse came in; now he must ration his bets. And so for the rest of the week he is a saint, a monk, disciplining himself under his new rule of patience, bleeding himself into position. He passed the bar once or twice, but mostly he just drubbed the streets round about, deliberate, refamiliarising himself with the territory, getting to know the locals: Jonty Orr in the homeware store, Indian John in the bookies, the two old lads who caretook the linen mill where the hipsters had moved in. Once or twice he gambled, strolled up to Beersbridge and round to number sixty-three, just to get a feel, a look. He glanced through the window as he passed, but each time received only the blue benediction of the flatscreen.

He frequented Beattie's, got to be known by Beattie

himself, son of the son of the original Beattie, fat as a friar, chips in his blood, whose patter ran comic, enlivening the dourest of evenings for regulars and occasionals alike. Here, has that wife of yours left you yet? Aye, actually she did, a few months ago. Silence. The pause, baps dangling in front of half-opened mouths. And then the clincher. Ah sure it's probably for the best, when she was in here she could never keep her eyes off me.

It was only a few days, but quickly he began to feel familiar. He found his tongue changing, the old gulter returning to his words, the vowels rounded more, the laugh at the end coming quicker. He tried out expletives in his head like Latin conjugations. *Fuck this fuck that fuck the other.* For the first time in many years he visited Abraham's grave, out in Comber where he'd been born. It was a tiny church cemetery, poorly tended but beautiful in the way of neglect. He sucked hard on the grief and guilt both. The years between insisted on their wastefulness. He is both having it and not having it. *Fuck this. Fuck that. Fuck the other.*

On the Friday evening he went for a swim in the Victorian baths on Templemore Avenue. Every child round these streets went to those baths as a kid. Fechner's mother would take him when he was very young, three or four, before she lost interest, or whatever it was. Then as now the small cubicles around the side, wooden shutters hiding bodies. Fechner remembered refusing to go into his own, and the embarrassment of her disdain, dragging him tutting into one with her, pulling his clothes off. *What's wrong with you?* Making him turn away and look at the door as she got out of her pants and into her costume. Stop looking, she would say. When he wasn't. The image returned to him, so forceful that he had to close his eyes, as though freshly reproached.

It was useless though, all this nostalgising, all this dragging himself around his childhood. He went hunting innocence and all he found were little shards, sharp wee cuts in the fabric of his life. And the itch remained, the carnal urge. He floated in the water and imagined Katherine astride Murphy, dangling over him in his hairy glee. Fechner had never cheated on her. It had not even crossed his mind that she would get the hunger herself. He had not known jealousy before, not in so plain a form anyway, and was surprised by the gratification that accompanied the bitterness, the permanent taste of iron in the mouth. You could get used to it. Though iron has its own demands.

Polio was in the bar. His face when he spotted Fechner come in, like a slapped dog, excited but chastened. He was with another man, older, wan. The man was wearing a suit as though he'd been persuaded into it. Fechner was struck by the long, lean face, gypsy-like, a rural tilt. He remembered a patient he'd had once, an elderly man he'd been fond of who told him he had aristocratic genes that took a detour. 'Some detour though,' he'd winked.

Polio stood up, opened up a seat for Fechner. 'Here let me get you a drink,' he said.

The stranger stared him up and down as he took his coat off. He was being assessed, Fechner knew, and tried to make his five nine five ten. Fechner wasn't skinny, but under such scrutiny his body seemed apologetic. 'Is that chlorine?'

Fechner nodded. 'I was swimming.'

'Should I know you?'

Polio returned with the drinks. 'This here is James Fechner,' he said. 'He's a doctor.'

'Is that right? What kind of doctor?'

'What kind do you need?'

'They that are whole have no need of the physician, but they that are sick.'

Fechner countered. 'I came not to call the righteous, but sinners to repentance.'

The man grinned, entertained, held out his hand. 'You know your text. Lenny Dunn,' he said. 'Butcher.'

'What kind of butcher?' Fechner said.

'What kind do you need?'

It was only banter, but it opened a door.

'And how do you two know each other?' Fechner asked.

'I work in his shop,' Polio nodded.

'I mean he's not operating machinery,' Lenny said. Polio was shaking again, jouncing the table. 'Jesus son for God's sake.'

Polio looked to Fechner as though he might perform for him a miracle. He had his hands on the table, like Fechner had had them.

Lenny shifted, clocking. 'Oh! You're the close-your-eyes boy.'

Polio blushed, snatched his hands back.

Fechner smiled, cautious. 'Some cures require darkness.'

Lenny liked that. They slipped into conversation, sipped their pints, murmured peaceably. They quickly found an easy familiarity. This Fechner's gift, of course, fitting himself to the circumstance. He spoke of his father – his illness, his birds, his disposition towards regret. Lenny nodded knowingly.

'If any man come to me, and hate not his father, and mother, and wife, and children, and brethren, and sisters, yea, and his own life also, he cannot be my disciple.'

'Are you religious?' Fechner asked.

'No,' Lenny said. 'But the shapes of the words are insistent.'

When Lenny went to the bathroom Fechner drew from his pocket a tiny box of pills he'd prescribed himself from a local pharmacy. He handed them to Polio, surreptitious.

'They'll help take the edge off. No more than one a day though.'

As Polio slid them inside his jacket Fechner said, 'And maybe you don't need to tell everybody everything, eh?'

He returned home on Sunday, strolled into his house head shaven and carrying ten rainbow trout in an icebox that he'd picked up that morning in the farmers' market in Killinchy. 'Galway was tremendous,' he said. 'Just what I needed. Look at this for a haul. How was *your* week?'

Katherine was confounded, unnerved. She stared at his head. 'What did you do?'

He revelled in her thrownness, her bewilderment. At work too his colleagues eyed him with hesitation. He felt himself rise to it. Where once ignored, overlooked in his blandness, a new wariness preceded him. One of his patients, an older man in his seventies in tentative remission, his pale, unconvinced face still blotted with cancer marks, leaned over at the end of a consultation to ask, 'And are you okay yourself?' Staring at Fechner's head. It was palpable, the small arrogation of power he had effected. He put Buchanan off for Friday drinks, pleading tiredness. 'Was it the fight with the lawnmower?' Buchanan asked him. Fechner felt something beginning, some louder voice within him preparing itself. His hand kept going to his head, the sharp cut soft and smooth and full of promise.

Friday nights were rowdy at the White Star Line. All the seats were taken when Fechner arrived, elbow room only on the floor. There'd been a march on, and a quiver of bandsmen shifted around in full regalia, white jackets and blue trousers with flamboyant gold trim. His nerves rattled. He spotted Lenny and Polio, and there he was with them, Rusting himself. He nudged his way to the

54

bar, ordered a pint, tasting the dread descend, the falter. He was startled by a gentle touch to the elbow. Robert Rusting's gentle touch.

'Fechner, is it?'

Fechner rolled a dumb nod. He caught in Rusting's face a barely perceptible stirring, like the agitation of fish below the surface of a lake. Rusting stuck out his hand. For just a second too long, Fechner stared at it, before finally reaching out his own and allowing it to be taken up, swallowed into Rusting's tight, firm, sober grip.

'I believe you know Lenny and Paul,' Rusting nodded across to the pair.

Up close, Rusting's hardness was almost glossy, oily. But evident too was his guilelessness, like a child given to cruelty but without the charade of adult disguise. He seemed, in his green eyes, in the movement of his face, to be delighted, though it was unclear in what – in the bar? Himself? Fechner? He ordered a round and Fechner assisted with the carry. 'Your friend agreed to join us,' Rusting said.

Fechner sat down. The threat of recognition pulsed live, insistent. He avoided Rusting's eyes.

'Doctor.' Lenny raised his pint in salute.

'Yes I heard you're a cancer man?' Rusting said.

Fechner had the dank, disturbing thrill of attention – he had been discussed already in his absence. 'Yes,' he said, 'at the Royal.'

'Filthy disease, isn't it?' Rusting said.

He had the momentary sensation that Rusting was flattering him, trying to impress.

'We don't get too many doctors in here,' he said.

'Yes,' Fechner said, 'they tend to stick to their own.'

'But not you,' said Rusting. Not exactly a question, not exactly not.

'Well, I'm not a stranger. I grew up round here. My father worked at the shipyard.'

Rusting raised his hands. 'It's all right, it's not an interview.' He slapped Fechner gently on the shoulder.

'While I remember, about Sunday,' Lenny said to Rusting, picking up a thread they'd been on before Fechner's arrival. 'Am I coming to yours or are you coming to mine?' Fechner sat back, took a sip, allowed the conversation to move past him, away from him. He noted Polio's calmness. The pills seemed to be working. Every now and again he would look up and catch Fechner's eye and look away. A vulnerable wee streak in him, a want, thought Fechner. Where a crooked stick will do, he'd still try to fetch you a straight one.

He caught the tail end of something Rusting said and pricked up his ears. He wasn't sure he'd heard right.

'Youse are family?' he said.

Lenny smiled. 'Don't go spreading it around.'

'You don't look like each other.'

'I should fucken hope not,' Rusting said.

'You be careful,' said Lenny. 'Joanna has the same genes as me.'

'Yeah,' said Rusting, 'but she avoided the ugly branches on the way down. No offence.'

'Taken,' Lenny said.

'So you're not brothers,' Fechner said.

'Praise God we are not,' said Lenny. 'He married my sister.'

Fechner scoured Lenny anew, reassessing, picturing the family album. They went on talking, Lenny and Rusting, making their weekend plan. He caught between them the finest sliver of equivocation; every now and again, and almost imperceptibly, Lenny would draw himself back, turn his head a shade, his sharp eyes fleetingly agnostic, before blanching whatever thought had briefly consumed him.

Rusting began describing some new shipment of gear he'd brought in. Evidently this was how he made his money. He had connections in Eastern Europe who would find him fifty TVs or a hundred phones or two hundred vibrators. All legal, apparently, at least by the time they got to Belfast. There were a few boys who worked for him, mostly young lads, boxers, friends of Polio's – he funded their training in exchange for a hand selling the gear door to door. Littlewoods, they called them on the road.

Cautious still, Fechner tried to loosen up, chipped in himself with a few anecdotes – some of the old student doctor stuff, bodies as punchlines – but mostly he held his tongue, watching Rusting, or not watching Rusting. Rusting's every gesture a gust that might undo him. A couple of hours in, Fechner felt the adjy nerve of the drink begin to take him, started to flirt on the odd slurred word.

'My time is up I'm afraid,' he said, reaching for his coat. 'Sadly I'm not a drinker.'

'We'll just need to work on your tolerance,' said Lenny.

'Give me your number,' Rusting said as he stood up.

Fechner rhymed off the digits.

'Good to meet you,' said Rusting. 'See you around then, eh?'

At home, with Katherine, the unspoken hung heavy. They circled one another now like animals newly arrived on the savannah that hadn't yet worked out which was predator and which prey. Fechner found himself disgusted, not only by Katherine's affair, of which he was now fully convinced, but by all the running around, the duplicity, the sleekitness. More than once he had the accusation prepared, but for some reason he was not himself sure of he bit his tongue, and again they turned out their bedside lamps and lay silent in quiet, treacherous peace.

On each of the following few Friday evenings Fechner surrendered himself to a late afternoon gym session before dressing down and taxiing across the city to the White Star Line. The workout got his blood singing, put an edge on his greed. It was Rusting's custom to be there with a few companions, Lenny on occasion but others too, regulars who enjoyed, if not Rusting's company, the status his company implied. He noticed quickly the ambivalence with which Rusting was attended, the carefulness around him. It was hard to say if he was liked, exactly, but somehow that didn't seem relevant, or necessary.

Fechner fitted himself in, quietly and efficiently. He had the patter down, could turn his hand to a yarn if the table flagged, but was as happy to sip away silent in attentive humour, savouring the new commonwealth in which he found himself. It didn't take long for him to become a fixture. Old ones doffed their heads above warming pints as he made his entrance. 'Doctor,' they would say quietly, as though the word conferred a blessing.

On one evening a fracas erupted between a few young ones. It was summer, an uncharacteristically roasting day. The bar was full early, a good crowd who weren't regulars taking advantage of the weather. The lager was doubly effective in the heat. Spirits were boisterous. There was nothing to it really, a few playful drunken insults that got out of hand, a couple of lads in their late teens messing around, a bit of slapping, jostling. One of them, not being too steady on his feet, lurched against the chair where Fechner sat, causing Fechner to spill half his pint over himself. The boy looked at Fechner with a mixture of disdain and confusion, like he'd had nothing to do with it. The lad and his friends went out the back to the beer garden.

Rusting had been in the bathroom, and returned to see Fechner patting himself down with paper towels.

'Well that's a worry,' he said. 'The surgeon has shaky hands.'

A bit of laughter around the table.

'It was some youngsters actually,' said one of them. 'Knocked into him.'

'Who?' said Rusting.

Fechner shook his head. 'It doesn't matter, just some kids.'

'Did they apologise?'

Fechner felt the old docility, the old guilt. He said nothing, stared in passive shame.

'Did they leave?' Rusting asked.

'They went out the back,' someone said.

'Marcus,' Rusting called to the barman. 'Would you go and tell those fellas I would like a word?'

Rusting sat down. The bar was quiet now, thick with anticipation. A minute later Marcus returned.

'They say if you want to speak to them, you can go and speak to them.'

Rusting sat for a second. His face refused expression. Every eye in the room was on him.

'Marcus,' he said. 'Tell them that's not how it works.'

Marcus paused for a second, weighed it up. He grabbed a tea towel from the bar and turned and walked back outside. In thirty seconds, he came back in, followed by the four youngsters. Rusting stayed seated, looked up at them.

'What do you want?' said the culprit, the spiller. 'It was an accident.'

'What's your name?' Rusting said to him, quietly.

The boy hesitated. 'Jonty,' he said.

59

'Jonty what?'

'What's your name?' the boy said.

Rusting looked around the bar. He tempted a smile. 'Jonty what?' he repeated.

Jonty shifted, suddenly careful. 'Kirkpatrick.'

'Jonty Kirkpatrick.' Rusting tried the name out.

Kirkpatrick's face twitched. 'Look it was an accident.'

'Well maybe you'd want to apologise then. Surely you'd think that would be the best idea?'

Fechner moved his arm, as though to speak, to defuse the tension. Rusting stopped him. He lifted his finger, then turned his head and looked past it, towards the floor, towards nothing, and waited. Kirkpatrick looked around, at his friends. He got no succour there. Whatever appetite they'd had for confrontation had gone.

Finally, Kirkpatrick spat out a sheepish, blunt 'Sorry.'

Rusting looked up, shook his head. 'It wasn't my beer you spilled.'

The boy turned to Fechner. 'Sorry,' he said.

'It's all right,' Fechner said.

'And perhaps it would be a nice gesture to replace his pint, wouldn't you say?' Rusting said.

'Really, it's all—' Fechner was again cut off by Rusting's raised hand.

Kirkpatrick turned to the bar. Marcus performed the operation, handed him the pint, took his money. He brought the drink to Fechner, set it on the table before him.

'Now doesn't that feel good, Jonty?' Rusting put his hand on the boy's arm. 'Isn't that the very best human feeling there is?'

At the end of June, before the annual flight for the glorious Twelfth when the middle class leave for Donegal, Murphy hosted a party. Fechner declined the invitation at first, just to enjoy the sight of Katherine's face collapsing into terror when he announced he'd changed his mind. Now here he is following her through the deftly hedged archway into Murphy's back garden. There were twenty or thirty of them there already, scattered around the large lawn. Murphy, in shorts, stood over the flames, the big rugby legs impressing. He fussed, commanded. He did not appear bothered by Fechner's presence.

Fechner picked up a beer and went and sat down at a table with Buchanan. Buchanan nursed a gin, neat. Katherine buzzed around officiously. Fechner watched them all watch her.

'You obviously know,' Fechner said.

'Know what?'

'Everybody knows, don't they?' He stared at Murphy across the garden. 'Why didn't you say anything?'

'James,' said Buchanan. 'What could I tell you?'

Everyone knew all right, but they had their breeding, their burgher manners. *Are there any classes you're struggling with son? Yeah, the bourgeoisie.* Fechner felt the longing in them for confrontation, for the big scene. It was a small satisfaction at least to deny them that.

'Do you think I'm a fool?' Fechner said.

Buchanan took a sip, gently set his glass back on the table. 'Show me the man who's not,' he said.

Fechner left early and took a taxi into the city. He knew that Rusting and Lenny were heading to a bout in Sandy Row, where one of Rusting's young boxers was on the bill. The gym was in Schomberg Drive, behind the shoe shop. He remembered Reids from when he was a child, being traipsed across town by his mother once a year for the requisite black school shoes and guddies, a pair of each, one size too big so he'd grow into them. His father's sister

61

Gladys worked there and was worth 30 per cent. She would ply him with attention to the point of humiliation. She had no children of her own, had never married, and treated Fechner like a pet, massaging his feet as he tried shoes on, letting her hand linger in his hair as she talked to Fechner's mother. He shivered as he passed the shutters.

It was crowded already when he arrived, pumping, filled almost entirely with men and boys, a handful of women high on the testosterone. The smell of sweat and cheap aftershave was factual. Fechner had never been anywhere like it. He'd drunk more than usual at the barbecue, and on the alcohol he felt euphoric: raw and visceral and alive. There was a fight on as he walked in. The ring was raised in the centre of the space. Fechner felt a shiver run through him as he approached, his hands shaking. The crowd throbbed with appetite, expectant, lairy. In the ring, two teenagers ducked and jabbed, tentative, describing shapes, putting out easy feelers. Through the ropes he spotted Rusting and Lenny. Polio was there too, standing mesmerised. As he made his way around to them he missed the punch landing, but he turned and saw one of the boys drop, floored, collapsing on to the canvas with a muted thud, the crowd suddenly electric, whistling, whooping. He turned to Rusting, and there he stood, staring in pure, feral rapture at the boy in the ring hitting his chest, his other glove in the air. Rusting with this barely perceptible nod: yes son, that's it, that's exactly it, suck it in and do not let it go.

They shook Fechner's hand when he reached them, impressed he'd shown up. Polio was sent to procure drinks. Lenny introduced Fechner to a few of the young lads, other boxers in Rusting's stable, there in support. By the time Rusting's fighter was due, the place was crammed, shoulder to shoulder. Rusting's boy was called Kenner, eighteen years old. As he came in from the back of the room Rusting leaned in, whispered in Fechner's ear that this lad was the real deal, a kid who could go somewhere. He walked in without a swagger, strolling casual, as though on his way to the brew. As he went by, Rusting reached out a hand and placed it on his arm. He looked up, stared into Rusting's bright face. Kenner was funereal, tranquil, like Jesus before Pilate. Fechner stared. He was another drink in now and felt his heart hammer carelessly, the liquor buzz smearing the edge of his senses. The boy's face was surprising, almost hypnotising; he didn't look like a fighter. He had fine, almost delicate, high cheekbones, like a starver's, quick little grey eyes, steely, imperturbable. It wasn't just what he looked like, it was the way he held himself, drifting almost, weightless; anywhere else, you'd assume he was stoned. Rusting let him go.

Kenner's opponent was announced and he bounced in like he was at Wembley. The decibels heaved up a level, whistles shrill, fierce. He was local, evidently popular. When the referee gave them the spiel, made them touch gloves, Kenner reached his out, but the other boy turned away, ignored him. For the first time, an expression passed across Kenner's face, a sneer, a satisfaction.

Both of them could fight. They shifted well, good feet, and threw quickly too, decent weight in the hands. By the end of the second round, they were both panting. Kenner still had that faraway glaze, but his application denied it. Instinctive, Fechner found himself moving as Kenner moved, mirroring the boy. Every time a shot landed he flinched. It was a remarkable sensation, something he'd never experienced, the smack of glove on skin like a drum beating in his own body, like his own body was a drum being beaten, finding its own relentless rhythm. He was

close enough to hear them breathing heavy as they steadied themselves, found their angles, ducked and weaved and
bobbed and parried. Kenner had a wild, swinging cross that
he'd missed with a couple of times already, that left him
open and tested his chin. But halfway through the third
round, he threw it again, right after taking a body shot, and
his opponent wasn't ready. The boy discovered it on his left
cheek and his head whipped around like a saloon door. He
tried to steady himself, but his legs were gone and down
he went.

It was raucous then: half the crowd were whistling their
displeasure. Immediately it was ugly. The ref was counting,
and so was Polio. Oblivious, no wit to catch himself on. He
had fingers in the air as the ref was going through it: one,
two, three, four. The crack of the bottle as it hit Polio's
head was brutal, the smashing glass echoing even above
the shouts. His knees gave and he collapsed to the floor.
The whole room drew breath. Even the referee turned to
see, and as he turned, it erupted. They must have been the
other boxer's crew, five or six of them, all youngsters. Polio's
hand was red already on his head, the kid who'd smashed
the bottle standing above him, almost surprised himself.
Rusting grabbed him quickly around the neck, brought his
knee into his face. The boy howled. Rusting yanked his
head back and hurled him on to the ground. The crowd
edged back quickly, and for a fraction of a second there
were just five lads frozen, staring at Rusting. Immediately
Rusting's young ones piled in, began swinging. Fechner and
Lenny managed to reach Polio, dragged him off to the side.
Lenny got him sitting up, put a towel on his head. Fechner
turned back to the brawl and saw one of the lads approach
Rusting from behind, another bottle in hand, raised to
strike. Like a dog Fechner lurched forward and crashed into

64

the boy's legs, bringing him down. Rusting turned, caught the lad with a clean kick to the stomach. The boy groaned and spat. Fechner climbed to his feet, stood over him. No one moved, no one spoke. As quickly as it had started, it was done. The two others still standing turned and legged it out the door.

A muted, careful murmur broke out, but no one approached. One of the young ones assisted Lenny, and they got Polio upright, arms under shoulders. Kenner jumped down from the ring, gown in glove. Slowly, unimpeded, they made their way outside.

The street was practically deserted. They made for a park a hundred yards up the road. They propped Polio up on a bench and Fechner examined his head: there was a small, deep gash. He whimpered at Fechner's touch. One of the youngsters gave him a V, asked him how many fingers he was holding up. 'Fuck away off,' Polio said, but he laughed and that was it, a release of tension, a wee lick of relaxation, the buzz of relief kicking in. Fechner had him hold a handkerchief to the wound.

'Fuck me, doctor,' Rusting shook his head. 'I can't believe that. Fuck me.'

'If we get him somewhere comfortable, I can put some stitches in,' Fechner said. He feigned to ignore Rusting's affirmation, fought to keep the grin down. Rusting pulled him in, kissed him on the top of his head. 'Who knew you had it in you.'

It was less than a fortnight later when Fechner's father took a turn. More than a turn, a major myocardial infarction. 'Who knew he had a heart to attack?' Fechner said to Buchanan. He was operated on before Fechner got there. When he walked in, it was startling: he lay there shrunken, tubed up and helpless, his violence pathetic, his jurisdiction reduced to a bed. Less than a bed, a button to call some young woman who would come, when she decided, and wipe the collected slaver from his chin.

Fechner asked him if he was all right. Edward's eyes were closed, he gave no sign of knowing that Fechner was even there.

Do I fucken look all right? Fechner mimicked him, throwing his voice.

'What do you want me to do?' Fechner said.

What do I care? Fechner warming to his own game.

'Do you need me to feed your birds?

Sure, you're so useless you can't even hold the wee fuckers can you?

'Maybe I should let them all go. Burn down the coop. Let freedom ring.'

You wouldn't dare.

'Wouldn't I?'

He leant over then, into his father's face. The smell of his body up close, the ancient filth, the acrid little perfume of his sweat. His face, unshaven for a couple of days, grey, patchy, unconvincing stubble.

'You're sick,' Fechner said. 'You are a sick man.'

Edward's eyes snapped open, and Fechner jumped back. They stared at one another, something live and shameful passing back and forth. A sneer crept on to Edward's face, disdain. But Fechner refused it. Remarkable to realise that it was refusable.

The doctor told Fechner he wouldn't leave for weeks. She was young, English, recently arrived. 'He's stable but very weak still. And vulnerable to another attack.'

'Aren't we all,' said Fechner.

'And I think you should prepare yourself for the possibility

66

that he might never be able to go home. He's unlikely to walk again unassisted. He needs care.'

'Don't we all,' said Fechner.

Not one for the humour, the English doctor.

'What made you come to Belfast?' Fechner asked her. 'Of all places?'

'Oh, it's different now, isn't it?' She was all sincerity, innocence. 'The *Guardian* had it in its top five getaways this year, did you know that? I sometimes think were it not for the murals you wouldn't know anything had happened here at all.'

He appropriated his father's keys, went to the house for a look around. A vague, colourless world up close. A television in a room without books, ornaments, pictures. No photographs of Fechner, or even his mother. The kitchen offered little more: tins of Campbell's Soup, tomato and chicken, a couple of ready meals in the fridge, a few beers. In the freezer, though, a box of Joker lollies, the kind they'd eaten when Fechner was a child. A big heave of naive affection caught him off guard. A life emptied of people, of love; reduced here to twenty birds. And still the persistent, pathetic weakness of pleasure.

The coo-coo-cooing took him outside. They'd sensed his presence, assumed it was Edward, their provider. Fechner could feel their excitement and hunger, desperate now after a day without feeding. But if he let them fly off, they'd only return. It would be easier, surely, to let them starve. He stood a plank up against the entrance to make sure they wouldn't get free.

Later that night though, Katherine in bed already, he slipped out and drove across town. Quietly, he let himself in. He filled two plastic containers with seed and carried them out the back, lifting away the plank, opening the coop, setting them gently inside. The birds juddered awake, hunger defeating tiredness. He had a Joker and watched them satisfied.

5

Once, Abraham, hunched over the cadaver of a young man only a few years older than Fechner was then, looked up from the boy's pallid, empty face and said to his nephew, 'Never get so used to something that you aren't prepared for its absence.' With pathetic insistence, the words returned to Fechner as he stared at Katherine hauling her faux leather Samsonites down the stairs, straining her soft back.

'You could give me something here,' was as close as she'd come to an appeal, and he wasn't sure if she meant a lift with her clothes or something more substantial, more personal. Surely he would, if he could. He always found her beautiful when she fought him, demanded something from him. If they could only have found a bit more of that. But how far do you have to go down that road to get somewhere new?

It was high summer, the first Sunday in August. The night before, either through guilt or weariness, she had finally come clean, blurted out the whole thing, and was disgusted when he admitted he knew already, had known for months, and had said nothing. He made no complaint, no challenge or fight. No, she wasn't moving in with Murphy, she said when he asked, but she wasn't staying here. Her outrage flared her nostrils and he remembered how much he loved her.

'Do you have nothing to say at all?' she said.

'I love you,' he said.

'Jesus Christ James,' she said. 'You don't get it do you?'

He admitted he did not.

In her absence, the house sucked the sound in and gave back nothing. He thought: this must be what the philosophers mean by zero. The first few days after her departure he ignored the gym and came straight home from work, immediately poured himself a large whisky and listened to jazz for four hours before going to bed. *Mingus Ah Um*, mostly, over and over, the sinewy coil of the horns around Mingus's bass, all that syncopated longing and disappointment. All that improvised *fate*.

But with Katherine gone the large house began to feel like an absurdity, each room its own testament to a failure deep in his character that he had naively thought he'd hidden, or escaped. He began staying instead at his father's. The thought of sleeping in his father's bed repulsed him, so he cleared out the box room and dumped a mattress on the floor. He would head over in the evenings, feed the birds, then listen to the same music and drink the same whisky as he did at home.

Work too bore out his humiliation. Every little glance, every murmur bouncing off his back as he walked past, all proclaimed his abandonment. Even the patients in their ignorance seemed to smell it on him, inching back warily, unconvinced. Buchanan tried. He would call into Fechner's office each day, and invite him out to his house in the hills at Craigantlet on the odd evening for a meal or a drink. But Fechner was not for comforting. He felt like an animal wounded too deeply, which must now be left behind by the herd to placate the larger beasts. He began to find a strange, surprising comfort in the company of the pigeons, which sickened him.

Towards the end of September, an Indian summer took. Two weeks of drizzle and dampness gave way overnight to a hot, dry weekend. It felt, as it always does in Belfast, beneficent. Rusting decided to host a barbeque.

In his reclusion, Fechner hadn't seen Rusting in weeks. When his phone buzzed with the invitation he was standing in his office staring out the window at the city below, the sun kissing his face with what felt like, for the first time in a long time, generosity, promise. He was not in a position to reject such gifts.

Still, he knew it was a tremendous gamble. He remembered, at the trial, Rusting's wife, casting her pitiless gaze around the courtroom. At Fechner too, surely. But his pain had something bright in it now, some wild little prick of energy that caught him and drove him on. Lenny found Fechner standing outside the front door, sucking up the courage – *number sixty-three, at last* – and startled him with a hand on his shoulder.

'Lenny,' said Fechner.

'I don't care if you're a doctor,' Lenny said, 'you still need to knock.'

Fechner smiled weakly.

'Where have you been?' Lenny said.

'Ah you know. Work has been busy.'

'He not busy being born is busy dying.'

'Jesus?'

'Close enough. Dylan.'

Lenny rapped hard. The door swung open and there she was.

'Joanna, James. James, Joanna,' said Lenny.

'Hello,' she said. She leaned in, kissed him on the cheek. She'd had her hair done: shorter, sharper. She looked Russian, Fechner thought. He saw the resemblance to Lenny, the way the bones fell. And Rusting wasn't wrong, she'd won the toss all right. She was older than he'd thought – closer to forty than thirty – but every bit as striking. It returned to him, his impression of her during the trial, the viciousness he'd fancied. He had to keep himself from flinching.

'Is it not Fechner?' she said. 'They all call you Fechner.'

'I tend towards Fechner, yes,' Fechner said.

'Well I feel like I know all about you,' she said, looking him up and down. He was ready to bolt. 'C'mon well,' she nodded casually, and led them through the house. Fechner took it all in, covetous. The wallpaper decorated with trees and flowers, a big plush sofa in purple velvet, unlit candles giving off a faint, sickly trace of lavender.

Out the back Rusting was standing aproned by a grill, meat browning already under his attention. A few deckchairs were scattered around, angled for the remaining rays. It was a simple garden, twenty feet long. Nothing fancy but nicely kept. A couple of their neighbours already known to Lenny were there, Colin and Carol. Introductions were made. By the hedge down the back, three young lads were messing around, playing some kind of game, darting back and forth across an imaginary obstacle, laughing. Joanna emerged from the kitchen and handed them each a beer.

'Thank you,' said Fechner.

He took a seat, settled himself. His heart still thumped too quickly each time Joanna passed her keen eyes across him, but nothing happened, and nothing kept happening, and slowly he relaxed. He gave the doctor spiel and the sick father spiel, got a few laughs out of the pigeons. Eventually, the food was ready. Rusting called the boys. They traipsed up the garden.

'Say hello to the doctor, Robbie,' Rusting said.

Robbie was a slight kid, delicate looking. Hard to put an age on, nine or ten maybe. Not fragile exactly but with a certain softness about him; his cheeks were bright red from running around. Fechner was startled by his eyes, green and expressive, alert.

'Hello,' the boy said.

'Hello,' Fechner said. 'Who are you?'

Rusting laughed. 'Yeah,' he said. 'Who are you?'

'I'm Robbie Rusting,' he said.

'No, I'm Robbie Rusting,' said his dad.

'Hold on, youse are *both* Robbie Rusting?' Lenny said, his hand in mock confusion on his forehead. They'd done this before.

Fechner couldn't believe it. His first thought was that it was impossible that Rusting could have made him.

Wee Robbie smiled. 'No it's me. I'm Robbie Rusting,' he insisted. He smiled and Fechner saw his father's grin in miniature. Absurd that it had never crossed his mind that Rusting would have a child. The three boys snatched their hot dogs and bolted back down the garden.

'The other two are ours,' Carol said. 'Wee scamps. Good kids though aren't they Colin?'

'They are yes, they're good kids,' he said.

Rusting doled out the adults' food on paper plates, while Joanna topped up glasses and dispensed fresh beers. The meat was delicious – Lenny had provided some nice cuts, prime beef, and Rusting was handy on the flame. They were content. The sun had dipped but still counted.

Fechner excused himself, asked for the bathroom. As he

73

climbed the stairs there were the photos of Robbie: as a baby, as a toddler, in P1 ... the higher he went, the older Robbie got. He half-expected that by the top the boy would have become his father. There were a few other family photos on the landing. He looked for Rusting's father, for William, but there was no William. To the left of the bathroom a door, slightly ajar, gave into a bedroom. Fechner paused, caught his breath. He felt his skin tingle. As gently as he dared, he nudged the door further open. There was their bed, a few skirts and tops scattered carelessly across the quilt. Carefully he lifted one foot and stepped forward, then another, then another. He stood in the room, silent, mesmerised. It was nothing special – an IKEA wardrobe, a shelf with a few knick-knacks, a chair draped with some of Rusting's clothes that he recognised. From the clutter on the bedside tables, it was evident which side of the bed was Robert's. He held his breath and climbed on to the bed, turned on to his back. He lay where Rusting lay, stared at Rusting's ceiling. He closed his eyes, let the darkness occupy him.

From the garden drifted up chatter, easy laughter. He lay there for a minute, two minutes, until the fear kicked in. He jumped up quickly and smoothed out the quilt. As he emerged from the room and pulled the door behind him, he turned to see Robbie staring at him from halfway up the stairs.

His heart thumped, blunt, implacable.

'I was just looking for the toilet,' Fechner said.

Robbie's face broke into an innocent smile. 'Oh it's just there,' he said, pointing straight ahead, correcting his father's friend, delighted to help.

Rusting put more food on. Fechner stood with him at the grill, enjoying the smell of the meat. Rusting was watching the boys intently. They were at the bottom of the garden again, occupied now with some game involving trucks and figures. Fechner saw his eyes narrow.

He turned to Joanna. 'What are they doing?'

She shook her head. 'They're all right, just leave them.'

'Robbie,' he said loudly. 'Come here.'

Robbie looked up. Carefully, he moved towards his father. He was halfway up the garden when Rusting said, 'Bring that with you.'

He went back to where the other two boys were sitting on the grass, watching on, silent, uneasy. He picked up a figure and walked slowly back up the garden towards his father.

There was a brief, terrific silence.

'Robert just leave it,' Joanna said. 'For God's sake.'

'What have I told you about that?' Rusting said.

Fechner looked to Lenny for a cue, but Lenny's face was stone. Colin and Carol stared on impassive, wary.

Robbie's head was lowered. Fechner clocked that he was holding an Action Man figure. Robbie shook his head.

'Where'd you get that?'

'It was a present.' His voice trembled, tiny.

'I can't hear you, look at me.'

'Somebody in school gave me it for a present.'

'What have I told you?' Rusting's voice all edge, no centre.

Lenny bit. 'Robert,' he said.

'This is not your house, Lenny,' Rusting said.

'It's my house,' Joanna said.

Rusting looked at her, then back at his son.

'What have I told you?' he repeated.

Robbie looked towards Joanna.

'Don't look at your mother, look at me,' Rusting said.

Robbie turned back to Rusting, lowering his head. 'That it's a doll,' he said.

'That's it's a doll, yes. And do you play with dolls?'

75

Slowly Robbie shook his head.

'Look at me,' Rusting said.

Fechner watched Robbie turn his big eyes towards his father. He didn't know where to look himself. He kept his own head lowered but watched Joanna. Her arms were tight against her body, holding herself back. On her face was a calculation. Her jaw tightened, but she said nothing.

'Give me it,' Rusting said.

Robbie handed it over.

Carefully, gently, Rusting pulled off one of the legs and dropped it on to the ground. He pulled off the other. Fechner stared, dumb. One at a time, precisely and without expression, Rusting tore off the arms. He handed the limbless doll to Fechner. 'Finish that would you.'

Fechner stared at the figure, then looked up at the boy. He froze.

'All right then, just give me it,' Rusting said, snatching it back. He ripped off the head, held it between his fingers.

'Okay?' Rusting said.

Robbie nodded.

'Away and play with something else.'

Off he went, head lowered, down the garden.

Gently, Rusting opened his fingers, let the head fall on to the grass. He tossed the limbless body beside it.

'For God's sake,' Lenny shook his head.

'Not your house, Lenny,' Rusting looked at Joanna. She stared back, fierce, silent. Fechner felt a strange knowledge pass between them, a sanction.

'I need to get some stuff ready for tomorrow,' Lenny said. He stood up, pulled his jacket on. 'I'll see youse.'

For a few minutes after he left, no one spoke. Rusting returned to the grill, flipped the meat over. When it was ready he heaped it on a plate.

'Help yourselves,' he said.

Relieved, Colin got up from his deckchair.

'I could murder another burger now in fairness,' he said.

More wine was opened, and slowly the tension dissipated, Colin launching at length into his opinion on Arsenal's troubles at left back. Fechner noted Joanna drift a few times to the back of the garden, with more food or plastic cups of Coke, and while there unfussily kiss Robbie's head, gently touch his back. An odd envy caught him.

For the rest of the evening the pieces of the Action Man lay discarded beside the grill. Fechner couldn't take his eyes away. He pictured putting him back together and then ripping him apart again.

6

Lenny had not at first cared for Rusting. When Joanna presented him she was twenty-two, fresh off a marketing degree at Jordanstown, working for Dale Farm. Rusting was a year older. She'd met him on a night out in Thompsons. He spotted her, he was fond of telling later, across a crowded dance floor, spinning to the music. Irresistible. 'Like a Minogue,' Rusting said.

Rusting even in his early twenties was a specimen. Lenny's first impression was of an oversized boy, one who'd been pumped up slightly too much, inflated like a tyre. Handsome in a way, but a little off-centre. He had an awkward smile: lopsided, tentative. He had the look of someone who'd been beaten and was waiting for it to happen again. That slight tightening of the jaw that warned you not to surprise him. But then he also had moments when he'd find something hilarious, and the awkwardness and defensiveness and harshness would give way to naivete and delight, his face suddenly open, his eyes flashing.

Joanna couldn't help herself. She had about her, even as a child, a pointed tenacity. She would demand that Lenny include her in whatever he was doing, even if it was too difficult, and she was dogged in her refusal to give in, persistent beyond the point of humiliation. She would punch him away if he tried to help with a heavy box or a bike chain that wouldn't catch.

And coupled with this she had an eye for the underdog. In primary school – only seven or eight years old – she befriended a boy who was an outcast, a grubby kid not much liked by her classmates. Lenny remembered his parents' bemusement, chuckling from the kitchen as they watched them play in the back garden, Joanna and her rescued creature, her determination to make sure he was accepted, made part of things. Even then Lenny, just into his teens, could see that she was committed to the boy not because she actually liked him but because she hated, absolutely hated, to see someone left out.

When Rusting came along, it seemed to Lenny – and nothing subsequently persuaded him otherwise – that something similar was happening. She saw not only the bravado but the nervy child of his father, William's only son, forced to create a version of himself that could withstand his surroundings. Everyone on the road knew William, by reputation if not experience. He'd spent a few years inside but was released under the Good Friday Agreement, and brought some of the brutality of the prison, or so it went in the rumours, back home with him. Not that he'd needed an education in cruelty.

Of course he was a child once himself, and no doubt there must be stories there that would season this one differently. But by the time he became a father, whatever might have been left in him of generosity or kindness had been emptied out. It wasn't just his propensity for anger, or his coarseness. There was a disturbing pleasure in the deliberate exercise of his power, in his threats. He roamed around seeking *prey*. Even in his younger days, he was known for the sick sort of hilarity he would bring to punishment beatings, the lurid glee. A few lads Lenny knew back then – wild kids but not bad deep down, just misdirected – took heavy beatings off William, many for innocuous stuff, petty offences. He shot both knees out of one boy for stealing a radio off a building site, because he happened to be friends with the developer. A shitty wee Sony. You still see the boy now, joysticking his way up and down the road in his little electric cart, tins of Special Brew in the basket, nervous eyes going like ping-pong.

Rusting's mother, William's wife, was called Sarah. She'd come up from the country when she left school, and met and married William before she was eighteen, grateful to escape the loneliness. Whatever she knew of her husband's activities, she evinced ignorance. She never asked him what he did, though she would have heard the same stories as everyone else. Even when he went to prison she was bluntly incurious, avoiding reports of his alleged crimes and shutting down any conversation in which they were mentioned.

They were not an affectionate couple. There was no founding myth, no story of young love that Robert was told. Never once in his life did he see them hold hands. He wondered, when he was old enough, what she got out of the arrangement. He knew she came from a tiny village on the border in Armagh and her father had been a drunk, because this was something William would say to humiliate her. He came to the conclusion that she enjoyed the power he had, the deference he would be shown as they went about together. It was enough to be with a man who could hold himself above others.

Robert was her only child. He was testy as a baby, needy but difficult: he would not take her breast. William had been in prison once already, for two years, and had come out with a deeper, savage edge. 'Would you shut him up or do I have to?' he would say as Rusting gurned, unsatisfied, and Sarah would take him into another room and try to soothe him, to little effect.

When William went to prison the second time Rusting was eight years old. Rusting and his mother were bemused at first, amazed to have such freedom. It took a year, but they began slowly to find a connection with one another, a shared humour. They each lowered their respective guards sufficiently that they could pool their solitude, and in doing so care for one another. Rusting thrived in this tiny kingdom. He found more confidence in himself, more assurance. He started lifting weights, swimming. In fourth year he was made captain of the school football team. He even began dating girls. He was shy still, innocent. From a distance you might have predicted good things.

When William was released as part of the peace settlement, Rusting was sixteen. Foolishly, he believed they could withstand the change, he and his mother. He felt that they were now a unit that William could not easily dismantle. So the sense of betrayal when she so quickly fell back into William's orbit, into his authority, made him bitter. He kept his head down, inasmuch as it was possible under William's eye, his appetite for confrontation. Robert was taller than William now, and bulky, and this reality – the fact of his body and what it hinted at, what it was capable of – brought into the air a tone of violence. William still berated him, demeaned him. But he was wary too, and Rusting marked it.

When Rusting met Joanna he was still living at home, working for a spark in Sydenham. It is not difficult to imagine the effect Joanna must have had on him, what she must have represented as both promise and escape. Their romance was quick, thrilling, propitious. She had an ear for his fears but the wit not to force him to articulate them. She began to open up tiny gaps in his hard façade. It must have tasted sweet to them both. And if she got the satisfaction of charity, of receiving the exile, she was not compromised by him. He was far more to her than a object of pity.

They eloped just a year after they met. Her parents were hurt, her mother especially. But Lenny had understood. It was the only way they could get married without having William there. It was clear by then that there was an animosity between Rusting and his father, and there was no way, not in their circles, they could have had a proper wedding and excluded him.

They'd been married nearly five years by the time Robbie came along. Not the easiest of years either. Joanna was isolated, a tiny, unspoken wedge between her and her sceptical parents. She was beginning to experience too the sharp end of being with a man like Rusting. If it was true that she had helped him escape, it was equally true that a history like Rusting's was not so easily escapable. He was relieved to be away from his father, but the anger he had felt there now bubbled under the surface, looked for other targets. Trouble began to find him. Nothing on the scale of William, but soon there were stories of clashes in bars, casual threats issued, intimidations. Ballymacarrett FC, the football team connected to the White Star Line, used to play up at Orangefield pitches on Saturday afternoons, and you would regularly see Rusting on the touchline, yelling abuse at the referee and opposition coaches. They'd been a good side for many years but began to get a reputation as thuggish, nasty, not a team you wanted to come and play. It culminated in a brawl with a team from Islandmagee, Rusting stepping on to the pitch near the end of the game in response to something said by their winger, who'd spent an hour and a half listening to Rusting's repeated taunting. That went to court – Rusting was convicted and given probation.

When Joanna got pregnant – less than a year later – she took to it like a calling. She was lit up, delighted. When the child was born, Lenny visited her in the hospital, and there was Rusting strolling around the room with the scrunched-up wee thing in his arms, his huge biceps comedic around the tiny writhing bundle of new life. 'My son,' he kept saying. 'My son.' When Lenny asked him what he was called, Rusting looked to Joanna. 'He's called Robbie,' she said.

Lenny at first assumed the name had been Rusting's idea, a standard little mark of self-aggrandisement. But it was Joanna's. 'He looked so much like Robert it wasn't even a question,' she told him later. And true enough, he did have something undeniable of Rusting about him, some rude innocence. Lenny wondered though too if she wasn't also offering Robbie – the name itself – as a sort of gift, a reminder to Rusting, an encouragement. *Here is a new person, with your name. Unbroken, gentle, free. Be like him.*

And so it went. Rusting played devoted, puttered round after his wife and son like an acolyte. The confrontations stopped, practically overnight. He got a new job with an electrical firm at the bottom of the Woodstock, mostly doing contracts, bars and restaurants and the like, all over the country, bringing in steady money. Around this time, Lenny was an almost daily presence, and he and Rusting became, of a manner, friends. With the edge on him softened, he became easy company, or easier.

Still, the first spring flowers are the easiest plucked. After a couple of happy years, back came William. Until then, he'd kept largely out of the way. He remained a big man on the road, but the Troubles were long over, and big men were smaller now. Rusting and Joanna lived less than half a mile away, but they were in separate worlds. William drank in different bars, asserted his authority among people Rusting knew but stayed clear of. Young Robbie had spent his first few years in a small circle, practically oblivious to his grandfather's existence. Every few months Rusting would meet his mother in a café for a fry, bring the child with him, but he never went to their house.

And then up strolls William, uninvited, to Robbie's third birthday party with a bike and a cake and declares himself. Asserts his position, his right to his patriarchal role. Joanna persuaded Rusting to let it go, to play along. William wasn't aggressive, exactly. There was always the possibility that in his age he was mellowing, and perhaps it would be easier and safer to let him in a little than draw battle lines to keep him out, William not being an easy man to draw battle lines against. Rusting, out of obedience or love or foolishness, acceded to his wife.

For a while it seemed to work. Rusting was careful around his father, subdued. Lenny, through luck or design, was rarely there when William was around. He did remember the first time he met him, at a Christmas party, Robbie four years old by then. William was half the size of his son, but Lenny was astonished to see Robert diminish, dismantle himself, collapse his bulky frame. Which seemed to satisfy William immensely.

The world teetered uneasily. Around William there was a bite in the air that made you careful how you moved, as though turning around at the wrong moment you could find yourself suddenly on the sharp end of something ugly. Lenny knew from his sister about William's criticisms, plenty of them as there were: the feebleness of Robbie's upbringing, the lack of demands put on him, rendering him weak, soft. To Lenny, Rusting would say nothing, but Lenny didn't miss the growing anger on him, the little twitch in the shoulder if William's name was mentioned.

It came to a head the day William took the boy to Kirkistown. A Saturday morning in August, the sun blinding already by ten in the morning, Robbie sat by the window impatiently awaiting his grandfather's arrival. Robbie loved motorbikes and had long been promised a trip to see a real race.

William pulled up at the house and smacked the horn. Rusting looked at Joanna then walked out into the back garden and yanked the lawnmower into brash life. Joanna brought Robbie out to the car. William had the window wound down.

'Look after him now,' she said as Robbie clambered into the back seat.

'He couldn't be in safer hands,' said William.

He lobbed the end of a cigarette on to the pavement. Joanna closed the car door behind Robbie, waved to him.

William looked at the boy in the rearview mirror. 'All right son, let's get out of here.'

When Robbie arrived home that evening he was buttoned-up, furtive. Joanna came down from putting him to bed and told Rusting that something was up, but Robbie wouldn't tell her. Rusting went to his room.

'Did something happen today?' He fought to keep the anger from his voice.

Robbie was under the covers, his eyes large and nervous in the nightlight. He looked away.

'Son. You need to tell me.' Rusting sat on the edge of the bed. 'You hear me? Nothing will happen to you.'

'It was when we were about to come home. He started—'

'Who, your granda?'

'Yes. We were walking back to the car past all the bikes and he said something to one of the riders we walked past and he said something back and then granda gave me the keys and said go on to the car and I walked on but I looked back and he was beating the man up. He pushed his bike over, started smashing it.'

'Smashing his bike?'

'Yeah, with his feet. Him and his friend.'

'What friend?'

'I don't know his name. Somebody he met there.'

'And you saw all this?'

'Yes.'

'Did he say anything?'

'When he came back to the car he laughed and said never put off a hiding till tomorrow that you can dish out today.'

Rusting stood up. 'But you're all right?'

'Yes. I was scared just but. I'm all right.'

Rusting breathed slowly. 'Go to sleep now.'

Within ten minutes, Rusting was at his father's door, hammering heavy, spitting rage. Years' worth of rage. William, on the back foot, tried to pacify.

'It was nothing,' he said. 'The boy's a drama queen.'

'You're not taking him out again, you hear me,' Rusting said.

William laughed. 'Grow up, Robert,' he said. 'And don't think you can tell me what to do.'

Rusting pointed his finger in William's face. 'I can tell you what to do around my son. And I fucking will.'

'That boy needs to learn about how to handle himself in the real world,' William said. 'And he'll not learn anything from you.'

Rusting returned home in a fury. He was off the deep end now. There were no more day trips, no more pandering. When Lenny saw him the next weekend, he muttered through pints, piqued, deprivating, warning the air. He railed at Joanna for allowing him to be sucked in, for going along with it, and with his mother for marrying the bastard in the first place. He bawled out Blair and Mowlam for unlocking him. From that point on, Rusting's guard was firmly up. Soon everyone on the road knew. A nervous, dirty little tension took hold.

Still, with William no longer around there was a brief period of calm. Rusting threw himself into work, sparking on homers alongside the day job. Through a contact he met on one of these jobs he began shifting flat-screens for two hundred quid a pop. Where they came from he never said, but Rusting soon gained a certain swagger, a reach. Regardless of the provenance it was good money, and Joanna, relieved that things were at least peaceable, turned a blind eye.

The road at this time was up for grabs. The flag protests had been and gone, and whatever else they'd done, they'd exposed a vacuum within these areas, a simmering resentment with no easy resolution. The old boys' power was seeping away. Rusting's claim – separate from his father's, secular rather than militaristic – was maybe, for a lot of people anyway, preferable. That's how it seemed to a pragmatist like Lenny. A new arrangement, a new jurisdiction.

A few months later Rusting was in the Star for a pint on a Friday evening. Someone tapped him on the shoulder. 'What's up with yer da, is he doing that for charity?' He had been spotted traipsing up the road in a skirt and blouse, wobbling on sparkly heels. Rusting disbelieved the account. But within the hour a phone was being passed around the bar with a photo. Sure enough, there was William in full regalia, even the lipstick and eyelashes, cheeks rouged for effect.

At first Rusting laughed it off. 'There's nothing that man won't do for attention,' he said. 'It'll not last.' But the next week William was at it again, and the week after that. He became a regular performer at the weekends at the Mermaid in Dundela. Rusting spoke to his mother. 'What am I supposed to do?' she said.

'You could tell him to stop.'

'I did tell him to stop,' she said, 'but he won't. Why don't you tell him?'

'Aren't you embarrassed?'

'Aren't you?' she said.

No one knew quite how to react. You couldn't laugh when you saw him, and you couldn't look away, and you couldn't say nothing. William's reputation was long and brutal, and for all his new-found fashion it still preceded him, still set the terms of engagement. William was aware of this, and he seemed to enjoy it, this aggregation of wary power. It felt *calculated*.

Lenny saw him do the act once, at a social in a bowling club in Sydenham. He hadn't known William would be there. Lenny himself had nothing against any man dressing up in women's clothes. Not his cup of tea, but it's a queer old world, and it did him no harm. Still, as he watched William, he couldn't shake an instinctive disgust, as though what he was seeing was less a celebration of womanhood than an act of revenge, an attempt to degrade the very idea of what a woman was. He understood why some people were enjoying it, but there seemed in it a vicious streak, a bitterness.

A couple of months later Rusting was working a late job

on a bar fit-out in Lisburn when Joanna called him.

'I know I know,' he said before she had a chance to speak. 'I'm nearly done here, I'll be home at ten.'

'I'd say it might be worth your while coming home now.'

'Has something happened?'

'No one's hurt or anything. I don't want to talk about it on the phone.'

'It can't wait?'

'It can wait, but I don't think you'll want it to wait.'

He pulled up outside the house just after nine. He found Joanna sitting in the kitchen.

'What is it then?' Rusting said. 'Where's Robbie?'

'He's in bed.'

'Did something happen to him?'

'Not exactly, no.'

On the dining table sat the boy's school bag. She pointed to it. Rusting walked over, undid the zip. He pulled the two sides fully open.

'Jesus Christ.'

Inside were four large bags of white powder wrapped tightly in clear plastic.

'Is that—?' he said.

'How would I know?'

'Fuck me. Where was this?'

'I found it in his room. It's his school bag. Well it was and then he started using another one this week, which I thought was weird. I was tidying his room and found it under his bed.'

'What did he say?'

'I haven't said anything to him yet. I was waiting for you.'

'I bet you who's behind this.'

'You need to go easy with the questions. Don't scare him.'

Joanna went upstairs. Two minutes later she came down,

followed by Robbie. He immediately saw the bag on the table. His face froze.

'This is very serious,' Rusting said. 'I want you to understand that. Do you understand that?'

'Yes.'

'Where did you get this?'

His bottom lip trembled. He looked from Rusting to his mother and then back to Rusting.

'You need to tell me son. Look at me. I need you to tell me where you got it.'

Still the boy wouldn't speak.

'Are you scared?'

He nodded.

'Why are you scared?'

'In case something happens to me.'

'Nothing is going to happen to you. I guarantee it.'

The boy took a deep breath.

'Granda told me I had to take it and look after it. Just for a while. Just to hide it under my bed and then when he needed it back I would bring it back to school and give it to him.'

Rusting looked to Joanna.

'When did he do this?'

'Friday. He was at the gates after school. I brought it home then and put it under the bed.'

'Why didn't you tell your mother?'

'He said not to tell anybody.'

'Or what?'

'Just. Bad things would happen.'

'What bad things?'

'He didn't say. Just bad things.'

Rusting steadied himself. 'Listen to me very carefully,' he said. 'Don't speak to your grandfather again. If you see him, walk away. And if he tries to make you do anything, ever – anything at all – you have to come and tell me. Do you hear?'

Robbie nodded.

'Do you hear?'

'Yes,' the boy said. 'Yes I hear.'

It was a Saturday morning, early October. You could have stuck out your tongue and licked the air that day, wet and close, a thick mist, intimating winter. Lenny had Polio on the counter while he prepared a delivery from the previous afternoon. Around ten o'clock, Polio poked his face through the curtain. White as a fish, uh-uh-uhing. Lenny wiped himself down and emerged to find Joanna, nervous agitation large on her usually blank face. He caught the stares of the few other customers, eyeing her with reverence and fear. He beckoned her into the back.

'What's up?' Lenny said.

'William's dead,' she said.

'William?'

'They found his body in the Connswater.'

'What do you mean they found his body?'

'He was strangled.'

'Jesus Christ.'

She looked around her. 'How do you do this every day?'

'Where's Robert?' Lenny said.

'He's talking to the police.'

Lenny narrowed his eyes.

'Oh, they'll want to speak to you too. Every bastard who ever met him, I'd say.'

'So they don't know who did it?'

She shrugged. 'They could line up half of Belfast.'

The police questioned thirty people that day, Lenny and

Polio among them, but made no arrests. In the evening, a coterie of family and friends sat in Joanna's kitchen, a jittery frisson at large. Lenny watched Rusting, who was calm though zoned out. Joanna attended his mother, who sat quietly in the corner of the living room as though hoping to go unnoticed. Words sunk off the tongue. The TV blared *Strictly*, absurd. When Lenny left, he walked past a Land Rover at the end of the street and received a careful nod. He wondered if the occupants were there for protection or observation.

For a couple of days, the road hummed with gossip. Theories ran lurid. Some feared the beginning of a feud. Others secretly wished for one, the chance to settle old scores, in the old ways. People started drawing lines, or imagined where they would draw lines if it came to that. Little bitternesses were nursed, coaxed tenderly back to life. Men glanced past one another on the street, eyes averted, wary.

On Monday morning two policemen knocked early on Rusting's door. They drove him to Castlereagh, questioned him again. Lenny heard that they'd lifted two of William's old gang too but quickly released them. Rusting they held overnight. On Tuesday morning they charged him with murder.

The next few months passed in a slow fug. The trial date was announced just before Christmas, set for the following March. Joanna told Robbie not to talk about it. In school a few of the stupider kids mouthed off, but for the most part even the hard wee bastards held their tongues, at the command of their own parents. This was not a family to get on the wrong side of, and it was impossible now to know which was the right one.

Joanna refused pity, refused too to be drawn into gossip or slander. She perfected a scowl for anyone stooping to innuendo or fear. Just once, in a moment of rare candour, Lenny poked.

'Is it possible,' he said, careful as a therapist, 'that Robert did it?'

'If he had,' said Joanna, her face a cliff, 'don't you think I'd know?'

7

Every year, just after Easter, industrious youths all over Ulster occupy themselves collecting every discarded pallet they can get their hands on, and through cunning, skill and sheer foolhardiness build huge towering structures, which at midnight on the eleventh of July are torched with gleeful abandon, flames shooting a hundred feet into the air, God himself warmed.

On occasion they reprise these bonfires, albeit at smaller scale, for Guy Fawkes Night. There was one such event on the Connswater Greenway. It was a mild night, all of ten or twelve degrees, balmy for November. Scores of teenagers arrived from seven, high already on lust and White Lightning, glow sticks draped around necks and placed like crowns on Rangers beanies. A few cowboys scaled the pallets, thirty, forty feet up, splendid and foolhardy, staking claims on poor girls' hearts.

Fechner was there, and Lenny. Polio too, with a few of the boxers, strutting around in their flirtatious prime, hungry for the flame. Rusting arrived, accompanied by Robbie. Fechner held out his hand. At Rusting's prompting the boy took it. 'Manners maketh the man,' nodded Fechner.

The fire was lit at eight. It took a while to get going,

flickering tentatively at first around the bottom, but then some lad chucked in a half-tin of petrol, and a whoosh ran through, and it suddenly caught, furious flames shooting upwards into the inky sky. The crowd cheered, a big raucous holler of delight. Fechner hadn't been to a bonfire for decades. He felt his cheeks baking, the roaring crackle of wood catching, some teenager's boom box pumping out murky techno. He grinned, surprised by his own enjoyment.

It takes a while for something that size to burn. As the wood took, beers were passed around, patter shared. A group of kids dragged an old sofa in front and sat down like they were watching *Casualty*. It was near nine when one of the boxers sidled up to Rusting, flickered into his ear. Rusting turned to the others. 'Come on,' he said.

'Where?' Fechner asked.

'Business to attend to,' Rusting said.

'What kind of business?' Lenny asked.

'This is no time for a strategy meeting Lenny.' He turned to Robbie. 'Stay here with your uncle all right?'

'All right,' said the boy.

A couple of the boxers were walking already.

'You coming?' Rusting said to Fechner.

Fechner wavered, stared cautious at Lenny. He was frozen, but a little volt of passion started coiling through him. Rusting walked off following the others.

'I wouldn't if I were you,' Lenny said.

Fechner said nothing.

'You don't know him as well as you think you know him,' Lenny shook his head.

Without responding Fechner turned and followed.

They walked brisk, urgent, towards Templemore. There was an appetite suddenly, a shared expectancy. No one spoke. Rusting had a determined air, and strode accordingly.

Like a general in a war film. It struck Fechner that some sort of confrontation was imminent.

In ten minutes they came to a little warren of streets just off the bottom of the Newtownards Road, terraces, former shipyard workers' houses, two-up two-downs. One of the youngsters pointed them along Tower Street, gave them a number. Rusting told him to wait as lookout. As they moved down the road, Fechner asked the other youngster his name.

'Beak,' he said. He didn't ask Fechner for his.

'So,' Rusting turned to Fechner. 'This pervert has been flashing wee girls again. They caught him at it earlier apparently. He's been warned already, but evidently he needs a proper lesson.'

There was no time to respond. They were outside the house, and Rusting had his foot up already and smashed heavy against the door. Fechner's heart popped. The cheap lock gave easy, the door smacked hard against the inside wall.

The place was mephitic. Every surface sticky, God knows when it was last cleaned. The bastard clearly had issues. There were food cartons and tins and discarded clothes lying everywhere. Mould thickened the air, fierce on the lungs. Beak moved through the downstairs, worked out quickly that it was unoccupied. Up the stairs then, Rusting leading. Fechner followed them both. He heard a bedroom door open above him, and before he'd reached even the top of the stairs a wail rang out. He arrived at the bedroom door to see Rusting hauling the boy back in from an open window.

He was a sorry-looking character, in his twenties but supplemented with an aeon of neglect. His beard was unkempt, coloured different shades of muck. He was barefoot and wore tracksuit bottoms and a sweatshirt, stained both.

His eyes were large with fear, bloodshot. Rusting slammed him against the wall, and he fell against it on to the floor. Rusting read him the charges – what he'd done, what he'd not done. He was whimpering now, a wounded animal sort of whine, sickening. It wasn't helping him. The kind of sound you'd do anything to make stop. Rusting dragged him back to his feet, slapped him once, twice. As soon as he let go, the boy fell again.

'What are we going to do with you?' Rusting said, shaking his head. 'Eh? What are we going to do?'

'I'm sorry,' the boy gurned.

'Aye, everybody's sorry. Those wee girls are sorry.' He shook his head like a disappointed schoolteacher. 'You like showing yourself around do you? You like people to see you?'

The boy hushed up, stared up at him with big eyes.

'Well, show us,' Rusting said. He threw his arm in a gesture, encompassing Beak and Fechner. 'We'd all like to see what you're so proud of.'

Fechner caught Beak's eye. A little unsteady, a little unnerved.

'Hurry up,' Rusting shouted.

He hauled the boy's sweatshirt off, yanked it over his head. He was silent, no moaning now, his terror concentrated.

'Come on,' Rusting said. His voice had a fresh edge to it, a new eagerness.

The boy dragged his T-shirt over his head. His chest was practically bare, almost pubescent. He was somehow skinny and fat at the same time, his ribs sitting awkward above the round paunch of his stomach. You could see marks on the skin, of carelessness or illness or both.

'Come on, show us,' Rusting said. The boy looked around the room, as though someone would step in, would come to his rescue. He caught Fechner's eye. He seemed to sense something on Fechner, and moved towards him, arms outstretched, face pleading. A brief flash of panic ran through Fechner.

Rusting stuck out a heavy hand and clipped the boy, slapped him hard, a powerful catch across his cheek, throwing him back against the wall. And then a shout came up through the open window. 'Peelers!' bawled the lookout. 'Peelers, come on!' Beak took his opportunity. He stepped around Rusting and punched the lad clean in the gut. He dropped with a blunt, awful groan. They hared down the stairs, the three of them, and made it out on to the street and up the alleyway to Templemore and then quickly Albertbridge, snaking their escape. By the time they reached the lights they were strolling casual as postmen.

A dark little frisson shut them up. Beak was itching with something he couldn't get out. He kept going to speak and then cutting himself off. Eventually he said he had to go and broke off on his own down Lord Street.

'What will we do?' Fechner said. He was breathless. 'Do you want to come to my father's?'

'We should just go home,' Rusting said. He looked at Fechner. 'Are you all right?' he said.

'Yes,' Fechner nodded.

'You're sure?'

'I said yes, didn't I,' Fechner said.

Rusting's boxers trained in a club near The Oval. It was an old warehouse built in the thirties, small, underneath the flyover, not far from Fechner's father's. Far from grand, it had nonetheless produced a few first-rate fighters, including a handful of Irish amateur champions and one lad who fought at the London Olympics.

By his own admission Fechner knew little about boxing, but Rusting began to bring him along. The qualifiers for the All-Irelands were a few months away, and Rusting had two boys competing. In his particular fashion he would hang about the gym watching the training, his presence both threat and encouragement. Fechner warmed to it quickly. The gym sang sweet: the air sweat-laden as he walked in, the musty, animal scent, the keen slap of gloves hitting bags, ropes floors. The trainer was an older man called Preston Blair. He had never been enthusiastic about Rusting's presence, and was even less so after the trial, acquittal notwithstanding. Blair had coached at the club since the eighties, even fought there himself as a youngster when it was set up as a way to keep kids off the streets and out of trouble. He took great pride in the reputation he had built for it in the years since.

He accepted Rusting being around because he put money in, decent money, which had kept the gym ticking over through a few lean years. Still, what did annoy him was Rusting's habit of pitching in with unwanted advice. Fechner picked up quickly on the tension, caught the old man glaring at Rusting a few times. He began, at opportune moments, gently to steer Rusting away, draw him into conversation about another part of the gym or another boxer or another technique. Blair noticed, appreciated. He started nodding to Fechner as he came and went, silent affirmation.

The space had its own energy. Fechner warmed to the honesty of it, its dedication to the perfection of brutality. The two boxers putting in the hard yards were Kenner, of the Sandy Row ruckus, and another eighteen year old they called Quiet McManus. McManus was the yin to Kenner's yang, all battery no off switch, his mouth as fast as his hands. He was always on his feet, bouncing up and down, mounty, jittery, spurtive. Put him and Polio together and you could solve the global energy crisis. He'd commentate on fights while fighting them; he'd wind opponents up by leaning into a clutch and telling them how pretty they'd been when the fight started but they should see the state of themselves now.

Polio was close with McManus, had told him about meeting Fechner in the bar, about the hands on the table, the letting go. Word got around. When he'd been there a few weeks, Blair pulled Fechner aside.

'I heard what you did for Paul,' he said.

For a second Fechner thought he was about to ask for drugs. Blair saw his hesitation.

'The visualising. Is that what it was? Uncoiling the turbulence.'

Fechner smiled. 'That's a nice way to put it. Yes. It's just a simple technique, there's nothing special to it.'

'Would you be up for trying it with some of the others? Help get them settled. Centred.'

Fechner was persuaded. When the gym had emptied out he sat McManus in a chair opposite him, a foot away from his own. Blair sat on the bleachers and watched on in silence.

'I can't believe I'm doing this,' McManus said.

'That's all right,' Fechner said. 'It's not like religion, you don't have to believe. You just have to do.'

'Do what?'

'What I say.'

'You're the boss.'

Fechner placed his hands on his own knees. 'Put your hands on your knees, like this.'

McManus did.

'Close your eyes.'

The boy closed his eyes.

'You're in a fight now,' Fechner said. 'I'm your opponent. I'm coming towards you. Can you see me?'

McManus started to sway in his chair, hinting the movements he would do in the ring. 'Yes.'

'I want you to fight me,' Fechner said. 'But you must remain absolutely still.'

'What are you talking about? How am I supposed to do that?'

'I want you to see yourself fighting me. I want you, in your mind, to move, to bounce from side to side, to pull away from my jabs, to lean in with your own. But I want you to hold your body – this body that's sitting in front of me – I want you to hold that body completely still.'

The swaying slowed but still he pulsed, a tiny oscillation.

'More still,' Fechner said. 'Completely still.'

Slowly the steadiness descended.

'That's it,' said Fechner. 'But don't stop in the ring. Keep moving for me, keep weaving. Look,' Fechner leaned in, 'I'm coming forward with a right hook, you need to avoid it.'

McManus flinched, shivered.

'Open your eyes,' Fechner said. 'Do you understand what I'm wanting you to do?'

'Yes,' said McManus. 'It's hard.'

'Yes,' said Fechner.

'Can we try it again?'

'Yes.'

It took three or four goes but the boy began to find it, to turn his body into a zone of calmness, of restraint, while his mind twisted and turned and fought.

'I've got it,' he said.

'No,' said Fechner. 'Now I want you to empty your

mind. I want you to let me move towards you and throw my punches and I want you to do nothing.'

'What do you mean do nothing?'

'Do nothing. I want your mind as still as your body.'

'While you fight me?'

'While I fight you.'

McManus closed his eyes, began again.

He left the gym half an hour later with a smile on his face. 'You are one strange man,' he said to Fechner, not without affection.

Fechner started working with Kenner too. Twice a week he'd take the pair of them and go through a variety of exercises, all rooted in the simple intention of turning the body to the service of the mind. 'What difference will this make?' Kenner asked on one occasion and Fechner replied, 'I don't know.'

But he realised that he could do something for them, that there was enough hunger on them, or desire. Blair admitted to Fechner that he was at first sceptical, but he saw it working, recognised some wisdom on him, some tranquil efficiency. It was a gift, the insertion of a tiny kernel of calm in the middle of the storm of youthful energy, giving the boxers a fraction of a second longer to make their decisions, to see gaps. The mind, stilled, opened towards efficiency, and ruthlessness.

Before long, it was commonplace to walk in and find Kenner or McManus or even one of the others sitting in front of Fechner, eyes closed, fists opening and closing like pulsing hearts in response to some instruction whispered soft from Fechner's lips. And Rusting, ten feet away, staring in mute wonder at the whole scene.

Fechner's mood lifted. He thought of Katherine still, but when he did the memory sifted as knowledge rather than pain. At work, among the bodies, he clarified. He felt his skill sharpen; the surgeries he performed seemed that little bit easier, his intuition purer. He sensed the separation between his hand and his instruments dissolve, giving way to the mutuality of form and action. As a younger doctor he'd flirted with Buddhism, if only for the recognition that the boundary between himself and the act, between the *I* of James Fechner and the knife, was an illusion. He thought of surgery, at its truest, as a form of meditation; the riotous, dissembling clutter of the betraying mind temporarily stilled, all desire reduced to action. No longing, no will; a body opened, corrected, restored, that life may continue in peace. He felt he was not like many others in his profession, their egos all bound up with the power of life and death. He was struck anew by the remarkable restorative creativity of his essential violence.

His father had been moved to a different ward. He had regained a little strength, could sit up, though he still couldn't speak. When Fechner visited, which he did every week, there would be a rotating cast of four or five other elderly men occupying the beds around him. The room reeked of flesh and disinfectant.

Always it went the same. Fechner pulled up a plastic chair, sat attentive and pointless. On one visit, he noticed that he would always position the chair just beyond the reach of his father. In case, one could only presume, he attempted to reach out and touch him. Fechner felt he was approaching something, a knowledge, or capacity. He had begun to feel Rusting's range as his own: a kind of gift, passable, transferable.

Edward's eyes were cloudy, weak; his body pestered devastation.

'Your birds are fine,' Fechner told him. 'I've been feeding them.'

Edward struggled to speak through the pain, his hand flimsy at his throat.

'It's all right,' Fechner said. 'I've given them all new names.'

Edward's milky eyes widened.

'You'll not go back to that house,' Fechner said. 'You'd never manage.' He paused, then committed. 'It's my house now.'

He saw his father's effort, to reassert something, to climb back into a position that he had spent his life in. The bitterness practically oozed out of him.

Fechner looked around, leaned in, whispered. 'Do you know I've been scared of you my whole life? Look at me. I'm nearly fifty.'

Edward did look at him, stared round and eager, as though he was seeing something new.

'Not any more,' Fechner said. 'Away and play with something else.'

8

As was his custom, at the end of November Rusting brought in a big shipment, a couple of lorries' worth. The Littlewoods boys hit the road with cheap phones and trainers, football tops and perfume, a couple of new-release kids' toys that had already sold out in the big stores. If you asked the right questions, you could also be sorted out with dildos and furry handcuffs. Rusting was no mug. He made half his income for the year in the run-up to Christmas. He had a book going where you could win a turkey if you spent more than fifty quid with him, and people topped up their orders to get in. It was a woman in Avoniel who won, and he delivered the beast himself, still alive, both he and the bird in Santa hats. The whole street was out staring at the poor creature tearing round the woman's tiny front yard. Eventually, when some idiot opened the gate, it managed to escape and took off at speed down the street pursued by a gaggle of screaming kids. It disappeared into the depths of east Belfast and was never seen again. He had to get her another. The second one he brought already plucked.

Fechner was helping him now: organising deliveries more efficiently, tightening plans for who was taking what out and when. The Littlewoods lads accepted this with some bemusement. One of them, a lad called Winkie Marshall, was in Lenny's, picking up meat for his mother. 'I hear Fechner has youse on a rota,' Lenny said, attention on the scales, not looking at him.

Winkie shifted. 'Aye.'

'How's that going?'

He shrugged, and when Lenny looked up the boy threw him a confused little nod.

At least with Rusting they knew where they stood. Fechner's authority was of a different sort. Ambiguous, implied. Still, in Winkie's reaction, Lenny sensed some reverence, or fear. Whatever Fechner was to him was in stark contrast to the cautious innocent who'd shown up six months before.

Bitter cold in the augurs, Christmas shivered. As the year ended, a blizzard swept in, the hem of the garment of Hurricane Sandra. When Lenny woke on the morning of the thirty-first, Belfast was pure white.

He'd never gone hard for the New Year. He could appreciate the ritual, the marking of time, all that sanguine promise of possibility and renewal. On occasion he would accept an invite, throw the glad rags on and head to a party, but more often he would observe it quietly; a walk along the beach at Crawfordsburn or, if he was feeling more ambitious, he'd drive north and sit up at the cliffs at Torr Head and watch the indifferent ocean.

He decided, this year, to climb the Cavehill. He knew Fechner would be on his own, and so extended him an invite to join, but Fechner declined. Lenny's head was filled already with vague foreboding. One of his regular customers – a literature professor over at Queen's (Lenny's meat drew in a high class of punter) who had over the years developed a real affection for Lenny – gifted him a collection of poetry, a first edition by Ted Hughes, *Tales from Ovid*. In the slack days after Christmas Lenny picked it up and was captivated.

He was no scholar, but he knew how words worked. He admired Hughes' restraint, his directness. And as to his subject: if there's one thing to be said for the Greeks, if you can imagine it then one of them did it. Murder, rape, incest, the destruction of the earth and the heavens and everything associated. All buttons to them, child's play. The atheists fear that humans are merely animals, but it's worse – no beast takes such pleasure in evil as a man. If you can't admit the depths to which any human being can sink then perhaps you're avoiding something in yourself. So held Lenny anyway.

The poems started haunting his dreams. He would lie down, hoping for Callisto, the Arcadian beauty. What man wouldn't? *Lust bristled up his thighs | And poured into the roots of his teeth*. It did too. *She wasn't the sort | That sat at home*. Lenny had never married, but the ache still carried. Still, it wasn't Callisto that came to him, nor Arachne, nor even Juno. It was Hunger. He'd never heard Hunger's story before. This lad Erysichthon had gone after a big tree in a forest owned by the goddess Ceres. He was warned not to, that the tree was sacred, holy, a refuge of prayers. When he first swung the axe he saw blood spurt out, but on he went anyway and hacked the whole thing down. Ceres was raging and sent for Hunger to enact some revenge. Hunger was a brutal, ravenous creature – face like a blue skull, *her lips a stretched hole of frayed leather | Over bleeding teeth*, that sort of fuckery. Ceres tells her to make Erysichthon's life a misery, make him desperate from the inside, unfillable. So Hunger goes to him and while he is sleeping she climbs on top of him and breathes into every channel of his body a hurricane of starvation. Immediately it starts to take effect – he imagines he's at a banquet, but the food tastes of nothing. And then he wakes up and sure enough, he can't get anything into him that satisfies. No matter how much he eats, of anything, none of it works, he can't get any contentment at all. Eventually he starts savaging himself, tearing off his own limbs to eat them. His own arms and legs. His last meal: he devours himself.

The thing was: in Lenny's dreams Hunger looked like Fechner.

It was freezing, but the sky was crystal. The moon lit the path the whole way, past the caves and then round to McArt's Fort. There were a handful of others there too, and they stood in silence and watched a few proletarian fireworks pop off above the glittering streets below. It was golden; for a while he forgot the heaviness, the disturbance within. The lights on the cranes sang covenants. From this high up, the city sparkled. Had he been sharp enough sighted he might have picked out Fechner, a stone's throw from the shipyard, slouching towards Ballymacarrett.

By eleven Lenny was asleep, contented with the night's early offering. Half an hour later the buzz of his phone shook him unfairly awake. Davy McTaggart's name pulsed through his squinting eyes.

'To what do I owe the honour?' Lenny mumbled.

Davy McTaggart was a customer, known well on the road. Easy-going but authoritative, and not given to needless charm.

'I'm in the Mermaid,' he said. 'You'd be wanting to get down here. Your boy Fechner is edging himself towards a hiding.'

'Fechner?'

'That's his name no? That doctor who's been hanging out of Robert?'

'What's he doing there?'

'Is he slow in the head or something? Just get down here and get him out. I've done what I can. You'd be wanting to hurry up.'

Lenny threw on slacks and a shirt and gave thanks to God he'd only had one whisky when he got in. The roads were quiet and he was at the Mermaid in ten minutes. He caught the stares as he walked in. 'We Didn't Start the Fire' was blasting through the speakers. A disco ball above the dance floor threw tiny coins of light on the dancers, cast the whole room resplendent. Still the violence hummed in the air. Half the room waiting for the countdown, but the other half for something else. He spotted McTaggart by the bar. McTaggart nodded towards Fechner's table.

Lenny made his way across the floor. Fechner looked up.

'What are you doing here?' he said.

'Put your coat on,' Lenny said.

Fechner stared at him. His eyes were glassy with drink but not stupid. 'Are you scared?'

'Do you think these people are playing?' Lenny said. He looked around the bar. 'Do you know who these men are?'

'I have been made aware,' Fechner said.

He steadied himself. He looked around and saw them staring. The Troubles are over, but there's plenty still to go around, if you're eager. Ten or fifteen of William's former comrades, faces red with drink and hatred.

Slowly, carefully, Fechner stood up. 'Well, all right, let's go then,' he said.

Lenny got him into the car. Already one or two of the watchers were stepping outside. He started the engine and sped off.

On the radio The Waterboys gave way to bells, announcing the future.

'There it is,' said Fechner. 'Happy New Year!

'What's that about?' said Lenny.

'It's when one year ends and a new one begins.'

Lenny looked at the road as he spoke, not at Fechner. 'You're out of your depth, James.'

Fechner brooded. 'You don't think I can handle myself?'

'It's not yourself I'd be worried about.' Lenny drove for a while in silence, following Fechner's directions. 'Left here,' Fechner said.

Lenny swung the car.

'This is me.'

He pulled over in front of Fechner's house. Fechner watched him assess it, pass judgement, secrete it away.

'I appreciate the lift.'

Lenny nodded. 'Let me give you some advice,' he said. 'Every time a dog barks you don't have to feed it.'

Fechner climbed out. He leaned down and tapped the roof of the car. 'That's good, Lenny. I'll bear that in mind.'

9

Fechner had a dog growing up, a golden retriever bitch he called Lucky. He got the dog when he was very young, a reluctant gift, his parents persuaded by Abraham that it would be good for him to have a creature of his own, something to care for and look after. When Abraham died – Fechner being fourteen then – Lucky was over ten years old, and had developed a condition that had her blind in one eye, with rapid deterioration in the other. Not long after Abraham's death, she acquired (in sympathy, Fechner couldn't help imagining) an ulcer. Eating was painful. She struggled to move around, and it became clear over the course of a few months that keeping her was tantamount to cruelty. Such, at least, was his father's reasoning. His mother by this stage was ailing too, confined to her bed, and the dog was just another cause for concern, another inconvenience.

Edward decided that she would have to be put down, but refused to have a vet do it. It should be Fechner's job, he said. It was a crucial life lesson, an essential recognition that all of life's blessings come with an inverse, a darker element that cannot be forever ignored. Someone has to carry it out – an act of love, after all – and it would be cowardly to hand it over to a stranger. Edward knew a farmer up in

Antrim. He drugged the dog with a piece of meat, and they drove up with it, the two of them, in silence. The farmer handed Fechner a shotgun as they lifted the dog out of the boot. No ritual, nothing to distract from the essential deed. Fechner felt a wild, bitter disgust. 'Do you want a minute?' the farmer asked him, and his father said, 'He doesn't need a minute, he'll do it now.' And he did. He pointed the barrel at the dog's head and turned his face away and pulled the trigger. He handed the gun back to the farmer and climbed back into the car without looking down.

Thirty-five years later, it's Fechner who's driving, sitting in resentful silence alongside his father as they nudge around the sluggish M3. The staunch, unemployed cranes of the shipyard still hang lairy above them, reminders or warnings, or maybe just lamentations. There is no drugged dog, but Fechner himself feels numbed, anaemic. Through his head flits a run of images from his childhood, bitter and melancholy.

In barely three months Edward had, from complete debilitude, sufficiently improved to be able to return home, a shock as much to his physicians as to Fechner himself. 'I don't know how this could have happened,' said the delighted young English doctor. Fechner knew all right, the fumes of his father's hatred a familiar scent. Still, that he had had enough remaining, and that he had found the will, the conviction of it, was a surprise. Fechner wondered if he had been faking for months now, letting Fechner get comfortable assuming he was done while secretly plotting his return. In any case, Fechner sat now in careful silence, delivering him back home. Edward ignored Fechner's warning that the AC worked better with the windows up. 'This fucking traffic,' he spat, as though Fechner had built the cars with his bare hands and sent them out on the road ahead of them.

It was March. Leaves were reappearing on the trees in Victoria Park; daffodils laid a keen yellow carpet beside the lake. Swans quarrelled over branches, stared at by daft, pretty ducks. Fechner had orchestrated a reduction in his hours at the hospital, which gave him more time to invest in Rusting's schemes. He worked only three days a week, the other four entirely at his own disposal.

His nights though posed their own questions. The sweats still caught, in the small hours. Jerking awake, he felt his body a stranger, his head aflame. In one dream, he took a thumb and pressed gently down on Rusting's head. Offering no resistance, Rusting shrunk under the pressure. Fechner snatched his hand away, and Rusting bounced back, a big grin scored blank on his dumb face. *Who are you?* he said. *Eh? Who are YOU?*

He met with Katherine. She had messaged him at Christmas and he hadn't replied, but when she reached out again, halfway through February, he wrote back. He was cautious, ambivalent to his own desire, wary of its return and what it might do to him. But he went and had lunch with her. He sensed her intrigue, her curiosity.

'You're different,' she said as she prudently grazed her way across a beetroot salad. 'I'm not sure how, but you're different.'

He liked that. 'Are you different?' he asked her.

'I'm sorry, whatever that's worth.'

She told him she was no longer seeing Murphy.

'Even with those big legs?' Fechner said.

Katherine smiled, complicit. As they parted, she asked him if he missed her.

'Well, of course I do,' he said. 'Whatever that's worth.'

Another delivery arrived, from Bratislava, but there wasn't much to it, thirty boxes of cheap plastic toys and a couple of pallets of laptops that were already too old to make much money off. They had talked, he and Rusting, of how to expand their reach. They were at the mercy of a list, on which, they suspected, they were at the bottom. A couple of Romanians on Jerusalem Street approached them, offering connections. They met them in the Asian Supermarket off Ormeau, walked the aisles among sriracha and ramen and chicken hearts. The Romanians made an offer, a proposal. Their remit dwarfed Rusting's current arrangement. Rusting was ready to accept, but Fechner urged caution. Nothing more than a hunch, but it sat sharp enough to prick. They held on. Rusting began to lose patience, fearing an opportunity slipping away. But sure enough, a few weeks later, there was a raid on a phone shop the Romanians ran on University Street. Five kilos of heroin were discovered wedged carefully inside a HP Dual Core i5 Tower. A bullet dodged.

Rusting was no ingrate; he appreciated the value Fechner brought. He entrusted to him more of the operations of the business, and the rewards. And Fechner took the money, greed such a handy pretext. Enterprise had its own charm too: assessing the opening for desire and fulfilling the clean need justly, quickly. It piqued the gratifying instinct. He began to wonder if all salesmen had had unsatisfiable parents.

The Slovaks had opened up a new operation, in the north of Serbia. Rusting's contact was a man named Emil. Emil promised, if they came out, to introduce them to some people he'd met, bigger operators who could give them more control of what they brought in. Fechner planned the trip; flights, hotels, connections. They would spend two nights in Subotica, where Emil lived, then one night each in Novi Sad and Belgrade. Neither of them had ever been that far east. The prospect of the trip brought its own excitement, a little thrill of anticipation.

But now here he was, helping his father from the car, gripping him lightly by the elbow. Both of them disgusted by the necessity, the reliance. Fechner had already cleared out the spare room in which he'd been sleeping, but still the house held signs of his occupation, books and records and even a little framed photograph of him and Katherine standing by Niagara. He watched his father take them in, assess. 'I can take those away,' he said. Edward nodded. 'Yeah.'

In the days that followed, Fechner attended his father. He brought him food, took his clothes to a nearby laundry. He had a stairlift fitted, and had the shower adjusted to allow for sitting down. He thought of his father's body under the water and was revolted. The image persisted.

He held his tongue each time the impulse arose to bite back at his father's sharpness, his lack of acknowledgement, his gratuitous disdain. After a few days, he arrived with a nurse, a Portuguese woman in her forties. 'This is Alma,' Fechner introduced her. 'She's a nurse.'

'I don't need a nurse,' his father said.

'Well, you do,' said Fechner.

'I have you,' Edward said.

'I'm not a nurse.'

'No, you're my son,' said Edward. 'Get her out of here.'

Alma picked up her bag and walked out, Fechner trailing angrily, passively behind.

A couple of weeks later were the Irish Nationals in Dublin. Kenner and McManus were both competing, in different weight categories. It was the first time in the history of the club it had two boxers in the finals. There was a mark on Fechner now, a warning. He was like a wound on the edge of reopening. But around the boxers, he refound some of his composure, and in sharing it, it grew. He steadied them; unknowingly, they reciprocated. Kenner in particular took the lesson, or the gift; you could see on him an evident change, a disposition shifting. Behind the glazed eyes now a keen tenet held, a menace.

They went to Dublin as a unit: Blair and his trainers, Rusting, Fechner, Kenner and McManus It was a bright, crisp Saturday, late in April. Clouds smudged a blue sky, painted, prettifying. They buzzed on promise, fists clenched against the cold, against the fear of defeat. The minibus dispatched the border with northern bravado. For the overnight they'd booked a handful of rooms in the Phibsborough Travelodge. As they edged past the Mater Hospital, Kenner leaned across McManus and pointed it out. 'That's handy for you anyway,' he said. They all laughed. All but McManus. Fechner clocked him: quiet, agitated, nervous.

They checked in to the hotel. It was early still, barely ten. There were bouts from two o'clock, but neither McManus nor Kenner were due to fight till after six, by which time Polio and the rest of the east Belfast contingent would be down. Rusting had a silvery, sharp energy on him, deliberate, audacious. Fechner saw Blair eye him with caution.

They taxied over to a gym in Ballymun owned by an old friend of Blair's, where he had arranged a final light session. Blair's taste in friends ran surprisingly eclectic. Barney Cooney was born to a farming family in West Cork. He had become a boxer by accident, in his telling, when he single-handedly beat the living shite out of a couple of boys who tried to break into his father's jeep at a heifer auction in Skibbereen. He still dressed like a farmer despite nearly fifty years in Dublin. 'Cleaner work in a pigsty,' he liked to joke, the accent laid on thick. Big voice, but still a good man for the background, which Blair appreciated. After the introductions, sure enough he stepped out of frame, watched quietly as Kenner and McManus went through a routine: warm-up, rotations, pads. And then Fechner stepped in. Cooney stared intrigued as one by one the two boxers took their positions on a stool in front of him, staring into his eyes intently for a few seconds before letting their gaze collapse into the shallow void.

'What's this then?' he whispered to Rusting. 'Is your man hypnotising them?'

'No, it's not that,' Rusting said. 'He's a doctor.'

'Well what's he doing?'

'I don't know how you'd say it. He steadies them, something like that.' Rusting's pride was palpable. 'It sharpens them, Preston says. Makes them faster.'

'Sharpens?' Cooney shook his head. 'Never seen that now, I must say.'

Over lunch Cooney cornered Fechner. 'So, you're the shaman?'

Fechner smiled. 'It's just technique. Bringing a little calmness.'

'And this is something you've studied?'

'Not exactly, no.' Fechner demurred. 'It's an interest. Maybe a disposition. I'm a doctor.'

'I heard that yes,' Cooney said, watching him closely. 'What use is inner peace though, to a boxer?'

'I'm not sure.'

Cooney shrugged. 'Maybe it's not inner peace you're giving them.'

The National Stadium was in St Catherine's, not far

119

from the heart of Dublin, just up Clanbrassil Street from St Patrick's Cathedral. McManus fought first. The northerners had arrived, almost fifty of them, and were boisterous, dominating the cheers in a crowd of almost a thousand. McManus's opponent was from Donegal, a tall, wiry, ginger lad in his late twenties called Patrick Doherty. He'd lost the final the previous year. At the bell, Doherty leapt forward, explosive, and threw a wild, open hook. McManus glided away, and it missed, but it seemed to spook him. He stuttered, on the back foot, his defence working okay but getting nothing off himself. In the corner, after the round, Blair cajoled him, tried to wake him up. Fechner stood ringside with Rusting and Kenner. He watched McManus, watched his eyes focus and unfocus, following Blair's movements, his instructions. But the fear was live now. Fechner knew. He felt the keen energy of Kenner behind him and had a sudden longing to turn around, to warn him or prepare him. But he kept his face forwards, on the ring. He'd guessed it this morning. McManus was done.

Fechner had never thrown a punch in his life. He couldn't have discerned a tactic, identified a combination. He barely knew how long a round went. But self-doubt he understood, he *knew*. And it hung on McManus now like a target. The second round followed the first, Doherty reading him, punishing. All McManus's bluff, all his cheek, was eradicated. Kenner stared on in silence.

He survived the third, made it back to his corner without a knockdown. Even Doherty's celebration was subdued, such was his dominance. As they stalked back to the changing rooms, Kenner put a comforting hand on McManus's shoulder.

'It's all right Manny,' he said.

McManus angrily shrugged it off.

There was an hour and a half till Kenner's bout. Blair led Fechner outside.

'What happened there?' Blair asked him.

'He was scared.'

'Aye well I know that. Where'd it come from?'

Fechner shook his head.

'Is Kenner gonna go the same way?' Blair eyed Fechner closely.

Fechner shrugged.

'Take him for a walk,' said Blair. 'He trusts you.'

They walked down to the canal. Kenner was sombre. The evening sun threw their shadows behind them.

'It was fear,' Fechner said. 'Why McManus lost. He got himself tied up.'

Kenner laughed. 'Yeah.'

'It's funny?'

'No, it's not funny.'

They stopped on Parnell Bridge. On the grassy bank on the north side of the canal, a group of teenagers were drinking, a radio spitting tinny hip-hop. Kenner watched them. Fechner was unprepared for this. Sure, he could get them sitting there for a few minutes, uncoil the relentless chatter of the mind, plant some tiny seed of attention, attentiveness. What had he done all his life but fit himself to the will of others? He felt a sudden disgust. He realised Kenner was looking hard at him.

'He wasn't scared of your man.'

Fechner waited.

'Of Doherty I mean.' Kenner spoke carefully, picking his words.

Fechner held on, let him take his time. He realised Kenner was working up to something.

'Rusting has this thing.' Kenner stared at Fechner. 'He likes getting beaten. He makes Manny hit him.'

'He does what?'

'He makes Manny hit him. He likes getting smacked around, apparently. They go down to the gym when no one else is there. He makes Manny slap him, knock him about. Sometimes with a stick too. He makes Manny beat him.'

Fechner felt himself weaken. 'I don't understand.'

'Neither do I. Manny says he gets him to whack him on the back. He loves the pain. Something like that. Makes him stronger maybe, I don't know.'

'Why does he do it if he doesn't want to?'

'Manny's done stuff he shouldn't have. Stuff that could get him locked up. Rusting knows about it. He's afraid he'll tout. I said he should just tell him to fuck off but he doesn't seem able to.'

Fechner looked away. A picture of Rusting flooded his mind, his huge bare back, crossed with soft red lines flowering to pathetic life. He shut his eyes. The thin squeal of Dizzee Rascal carried up from the bank. A dog barked furiously. Fechner thought of his father, imagined him lying face down on the floor in his house, unable to get up, unattended.

'Does Rusting hit him back?' Fechner said.

'No. He just likes getting hit,' Kenner said. 'Don't say anything to him. To either of them.'

Fechner stared at him. No fear on Kenner, remarkably. His languid, sleepy manner, it struck Fechner for the first time, was just a holder, a disguise. He sensed, as he had not before, Kenner's remarkable capacity for violence, both the giving and the receiving.

'Does anyone else know?'

'Polio. Nobody else I don't think. Look, I won't be scared

in my fight,' Kenner said. 'That's why we're here, right? You and me?'

Fechner said nothing.

'I don't need anything,' Kenner went on. 'Just help me focus before and let me go. I'll do what I need to. I'll win or I won't, but if I lose it won't be because I'm scared.'

As they stood there a heron dropped, suddenly, on to a log on the canal below, not twenty feet away. It flapped its wings, shook itself out, stood to attention. It looked one way, then the other. Even the teenagers turned, paused. One of them reached for the stereo, slapped it off. For a second they stood, all of them, in reverent, dumb stillness, staring. The sounds of the city were a form of silence, even praise. And then the bird raised its head, proud, and bent its legs and took off, low on the water, west into the hazy sun.

Kenner struggled at the start, stepped too easily onto his opponent's fists. He'd worked with Blair on his open guard, a risk in one direction that funded an opportunity in another, allowing him to move his upper body deceptively swift, unleash his own punches. But it wasn't working. His opponent was from Dublin, a young Nigerian called Emem Okoye, taller than Kenner and with a longer reach. Kenner's plan was to get in and out, land and go, but everything he connected with cost him on the way back. The first round went comfortable to Okoye. The local crowd, determined to be cosmopolitan, urged on their adopted citizen. In the corner, Blair paid out his admonitions. Kenner sucked on the bottle. He shook his head. 'It's not working.'

Blair hesitated. 'Stick to the plan,' he said. The bell rang.

For another minute, it went the same. Kenner doubled down, to bland effect. Okoye picked him off, scored every three for Kenner's two. Fechner watched Blair blanch, dismay. And then Kenner shifted, stepped inside and instead of pulling back out took a punch and leaned in closer. Momentarily, Okoye dithered. Kenner landed a hard, clean body shot, and Okoye felt it. Now he tried to step out, but Kenner didn't let him, he stayed with him, inside the reach, allowing Okoye to throw, even to catch him, but getting off little runs of punches now, all to the body. Okoye threw heavy, trying to shake him off, but Kenner took them and kept popping off flurries, one-two-three-four. The bell rang. Kenner sat down on the stool, sweat pouring off him. 'Do you have another one of those in you?' Blair asked him. Kenner winced. 'One way to find out.'

In the third round, the casual Kenner disappeared, the languid ease suddenly explosive. He went inside again, like before, and just as Okoye reacted, he pulled back, dancing. Kenner began to catch him at reach, Okoye wavering now, uncertain. With a minute to go, Kenner dived in again and stayed, and Okoye had no answer. He pulled his arms in to protect his ribs, and for the first time in the fight Kenner threw an uppercut and connected perfectly with his chin. Okoye dropped. He got to his feet again within the count, but the fight was done. When the bell went twenty seconds later, Kenner stood still, poised, careful. Okoye stepped to him with grace and hugged him, and Kenner accepted it and kissed the boy's neck.

The northerners took to the streets, enlarged the victory with drink. Fechner watched McManus, who hung back, subdued among the raucous crew. He watched Rusting too; pulsing, driving the revelry. Hands deep in deep pockets he doled out pints, floating back and forth between the elders and the teenagers bent on carousal.

Midnight found them rowdy in the Porterhouse. Final stouts downed, Polio and the juveniles grabbed their bags for the late-night bus. McManus stood up too.

'Where are you going?' Rusting asked him.

'I'm gonna go back with these ones,' McManus said.

'Sure, your stuff's in the hotel,' Rusting said.

McManus wavered. Polio stared at the ground, his hands twitching by his sides. Fechner sensed the impotent rage on him.

'You shouldn't feel bad because you lost,' Rusting said. He was drunk. He might have been attempting kindness. 'You made it this far.'

Kenner caught Fechner's eye, shook his head, barely perceptible.

'All right well,' Polio said, his voice careful. 'We need to go here to get the half twelve.'

'We'll bring your stuff back tomorrow,' Fechner ventured, as offhand as he could manage. He looked around as though to find Kenner, and found him. 'You can bring his bag back, right?'

McManus stared at him, quizzical. Polio too, eyes narrowed, uncertain. Beside him, Fechner felt Rusting shrug.

The youngsters left, McManus with them. Fechner watched Polio's hand go to McManus's shoulder on the way out.

'Must be your round,' said Rusting to Fechner.

A week after the fight, McManus went to ground. Word was he'd gone to London. No one knew where exactly, or why. Or whether he'd be back. Kenner played the innocent. He already, Fechner sensed, regretted what he'd given up. He wore his ignorance wry though, stubborn, even around Rusting. The title, it seemed, amplified his confidence.

Fechner did what Fechner had always done: he gave himself to the call of the body. In theatre he parted chests, meticulous, made sufferers well through sundering. The irony returned to him: it was division that made whole, the separation of the spotless from the blemished. *Go forth and multiply* was the claim of death, the song of the virus. The old vindication remained, his skills at the service of the people. Still, even expertise was a mean distraction. He could find no place where Rusting was not. At work, at home, at his father's – in every street and every alleyway, Rusting loomed over him, his live flesh a relentless demand on Fechner's imagination. *Could you call it sickness?* Fechner's inner voice harangued him. *Well what else would you call it?* Sitting in the Star, drinking and holding court, Rusting's bravado began to look like a posture. Where before Fechner had seen nothing but conviction, he began to read artifice; where toughness, deficiency. An afflictive little seed of doubt took root, sprouted in Fechner. He refused it water, refused it air; still it grew. He recalled another story Abraham told him, about a man who went seeking the source of the sun. Each day he would get up and start walking in the direction he'd seen it rise. Every day feeling he must be getting closer, until he realised he was back where he started. The sun rises inside you, Abraham counselled. Fechner was not comforted.

10

The weekend before their trip to Serbia, Joanna threw a surprise birthday party for Lenny, for his fiftieth. They gathered, almost thirty of them, in Rusting's dining room, and as Lenny landed gullible for a fraternal beer they pounced, announced themselves in raucous terms, poppers and streamers, yeeeeooooooows declarative. Young Robbie swung accurate with a water cannon, caught his uncle clean. Half the room clean, in fact. That was brought to an end swift. Still, all in good humour.

Rusting and Joanna played out the welcomes, but Fechner caught now between them a new precariousness. It wasn't much, just a little something awkward at the edge of their exchanges, a spareness. Every time Rusting spoke to Joanna, Fechner saw caution, absent the authority with which he commanded elsewhere. Once Fechner had a hold of it, it was all he could see, Rusting's soft eyes pleading permission as his mouth mimicked demand.

In the kitchen, he heaped his plate. Lenny sidled up. He clinked his bottle against Fechner's glass.

'Happy birthday,' Fechner said.

'I appreciate that.' Lenny threw some sausage rolls into a paper bowl. 'Are you ready for your jaunt?' he said.

'More or less,' Fechner said.

Lenny knocked back a gulp. 'What are you after?'

'We're just wanting to expand the inventory, find a more consistent supplier. We need to—'

'No, I mean,' Lenny leaned in, his finger gentle to Fechner's chest. 'What are *you* after?' He narrowed his eyes.

Lenny was drunk. Still, Fechner felt a little scamper of fear, then, as quickly, replacing it, a surge of rage. His jaw tightened.

Lenny saw it. 'Well,' he said, pulling away. 'I do hope it's very successful for youse.'

They touched down in Budapest at nine in the evening. Emil had promised to send someone to collect them, and sure enough in arrivals, among the iPad displayers, was a young man in a once-navy PSG tracksuit holding a piece of paper with 'RUSTING' scrawled semi-legibly. He was maybe nineteen, twenty. His careless fair hair was cut short, his small blue eyes impassive. Rusting approached him. He turned the paper towards himself as though it might now contain a picture to compare against.

'You are Rusting?' he said. 'The Irish?'

'Close enough,' Rusting grinned.

The boy looked confused.

'Yes,' Rusting said. 'Me Rusting, him Fechner.'

The boy stared at them without opinion. 'Come.' He turned and led them out of the airport. He walked quickly, purposefully. Soft on his feet, as though he might at any moment break into a run.

'Are we in a hurry?' Rusting called to him.

'A hurry? No hurry.' For the first time the boy smiled. 'Is far, two hours, two and a half.'

Rusting turned to Fechner, raised his eyebrows.

They drove south. Fechner sat in the back. The boy drove quickly, confidently. On the stereo seemed to be some kind of live comedy, judging by the laughter. For a while, no one spoke.

'What is your name?' Rusting said, eventually.

'My name is Ivo.'

'You live in Subotica?'

'Yes,' he said.

Rusting tried to get a conversation going. 'And you work for Emil?'

'Emil?' He seemed confused. Then he realised, laughed, corrected Rusting's pronunciation. 'Yes, I work for Emil. Just to drive.'

'You are a boxer?'

Fechner had been staring out the window at the blur of Hungary. He glanced round, first at Rusting, then in the mirror at the boy.

'Boxer?' the boy said.

'Boxer. Like fighter.' Rusting threw a little one-two into the air in front of him.

Ivo laughed. 'No, not boxer,' he said.

Rusting turned to Fechner. 'Doesn't he remind you of McManus?'

The sun set as they passed Kecskemét on their left, just sixty miles from the Serbian border. The sky shifted pink, pinker. Electric lights popped on overhead as they passed under. An hour later, Ivo dropped them at the hotel. Fechner, exhausted, collapsed into a sofa in the lobby as Rusting checked in. A few minutes later, he returned.

'They made a balls-up. They only have one room.'

'Only one,' Fechner said.

'It has two beds,' Rusting said. 'They can give us another one tomorrow.'

'All the others are taken?'

'Yeah. Sure it's only one night.'

Fechner clambered slowly to his feet.

'Sure you're knackered,' Rusting said. 'You'll be out in no time.'

They followed a porter up the lift and down a long corridor.

He opened the door for them. 'Is okay?' he said.

There were two single beds five feet apart. A thin scent of ammonia hung in the thick air.

'Dandy,' Rusting said.

Fechner performed his ablutions. When he emerged from the bathroom, Rusting was already in bed.

'Some day, eh?' Rusting said, cheerful.

When Fechner too was tucked up, he turned the light out. After a couple of minutes though, Rusting sat upright. 'Fuck sake I forgot to clean my teeth,' he said. He climbed out of bed, rummaged in his luggage. Fechner stared at the rough form scrabbling on the floor before him. Rusting, kneeling over his suitcase, his blank back huge. Hints, warnings of lines patterned across it, stinging through the blackness. Fechner stared as long as he dared, uncertain still. Rusting found what he was looking for, stood up and stepped into the bathroom.

When he returned to bed, Rusting fell asleep quickly. Fechner lay listening to his steady breathing. His own heart caught the rhythm, beat along in conviction, in protest. A vague trepidation gripped him. He tried to sort out his thoughts, but they tumbled, one on top of the other, into a fevered confusion. Overpowering them all, the promise, the insistence, of Rusting's back, soft and wealed, slowly healing under a thin cotton sheet.

He lay there an hour, two hours. Sleep resolutely refused

to come. Fechner could have wept. At three in the morning, he silently rose. He stepped towards the bathroom, paused. He assessed Rusting's droning rasp, the gentle heave of his lungs, undisturbed. He took one step towards him, then another. Fechner's eyes adjusted to the faint, desperate light. Rusting slept on his front, arms by his side, like a child. Fechner stood above him now. With a surgeon's touch he took hold of the cotton sheet, drew it delicately down. He waited for the breathing to give, but it didn't. He pulled further, one inch, another. There they were, doubt dispelled, thin red lines, like the tracks of ants across a forest floor. Soon Rusting's whole back was before him. It betrayed the violence he'd received, the violence he'd sought. More: it announced his weakness, his appetite for subjugation, for submission. Fechner felt the revulsion, the dull, bitter disenthrall. He used the bathroom, returned to his bed. When sleep did come, it came with wrath, with unsparing malice. In his dream, his father walks in on him as he dresses. His father laughs, an uproar, a fit, choking on it. *Ha ha ha ha ha ha.* Fechner first angry, then confused, then, finally, stunned to realise that he is laughing because Fechner has put on – unaware, unchosen surely, tricked! – his mother's clothes.

Emil was awaiting them in the lobby the following morning. In the photos they'd seen of him he had a homely, supple look, like a farm labourer from a family of farm labourers. Wry, even wholesome. But in real life he was fleshier, chubby even. His eyes were flat, sterile, distant. He smiled though and greeted them.

Ivo drove. Emil spoke to the mirror, outlined the plan. There were two sets of people he would introduce them to today, and one tomorrow in Novi Sad.

'And Belgrade?' Fechner asked.

Emil waved his hand. He turned to face them in the back. 'No Belgrade, he is out of action.'

'Out of action?' Rusting asked.

He grinned, his eyes sparking into brief life. 'He is in prison.'

The first visit went poorly. Emil took them to a warehouse in the south, outside the city, well away from the beautiful, stately churches and clean, colourful downtown hotels. Torn fences and rubble surrounded a grubby industrial estate. Ivo waited in the car. They were met at the entrance by two men in their sixties, unenthusiastic. They followed them around a huge, windowless storeroom filled with cheap, poorly made electronics. Rusting and Fechner barely said a word. Fechner saw the confusion on Rusting, the disappointment, but waited for him to take the lead. Emil saw it too. Halfway round the room he spoke sharply to the two men in Serbian. They stared at him, shrugged.

He turned to Rusting. 'This is not what you want, yes?'

'No,' Rusting said. 'I can't sell this.'

Fechner caught the bitterness on him but also, in his petulance, the sense that he was out of his depth.

Back in the car, Emil apologised. 'They are new,' he said. 'I not work with them already. A friend, he told me about them.'

Fechner appeased. 'What about the others?'

'The others are good. Tonight, and tomorrow, you will see. I know them, I work with them. You will see.'

He dropped them back to the hotel, promised to collect them later for the second meeting. They spent the afternoon wandering the streets downtown. It was pretty, but Rusting was not in the mood to sightsee. He muttered still, aggrieved, sour. Fechner was careful to appear upbeat. He pushed the thought of Rusting's weakness from his mind.

As they scoured the avenues, he walked in front so that he would not see Rusting's back and be forced to dwell on it.

Emil turned up at five, this time without Ivo. He drove them across the city to the western suburbs. The houses increased in size if not in charm. Outside one, Emil pulled the car over, leaned out and announced himself to an electronic box by the gate. After a moment, the gate swung smoothly, remotely open, and they drove into a large courtyard.

The house was two storeys, nondescript, featureless save for a balcony on the first floor that wrapped around one corner, on which sat a few lonely pieces of furniture. It was hard to imagine it happily occupied. The exterior walls were washed in a dull, unwelcoming grey, but Fechner felt it deliberate, from choice rather than neglect or poor taste. The camouflage of blandness.

They were welcomed by a housekeeper, a young woman who introduced herself as Maja. She was brisk, efficient, spoke English well with a TV accent. She led them into a sitting room, offered them something to drink. Fechner accepted tea, Rusting a beer. The smell of meat cooking somewhere nearby caught on their throats, sapid. It made Fechner long for salt. They waited in silence as Maja disappeared to a distant kitchen. Fechner looked around the room, noted the mid-century furniture, Scandinavian, impressively understated and undoubtedly expensive. The sofa and armchair were comfortable, finely covered. On the walls hung three or four pieces of art, abstract, sexual, showy. They were the only hint at an insecurity of style.

Emil had filled them in on the way over. Mladen Petrović was somewhere between fifty and sixty years old, depending on who you asked. He was shrewd, ambitious, wilful. This was Fechner's impression, reading between the simpler

133

lines of Emil's account, in which he was a poor country boy who came to the city and, through enterprise and talent and an eye for a bargain, had made himself into a wealthy man, first in Belgrade and now here in Subotica. Violence, though, hung unspoken at the edge of Emil's assessment, ruthlessness. Emil had worked with Petrović for some years when he'd lived in Bratislava, shifting goods for him, acting as a middleman with resellers further west. For a couple of years Emil had even lived in Germany on Petrović's dollar, trying, with limited success, to open avenues there. He was a hard man but fundamentally kind, Emil emphasised, so much so that Fechner could only doubt it.

He kept them waiting. They had almost finished their drinks when he finally appeared. He wasn't tall, maybe five foot six, compact, with thick, curly hair, greying carelessly. He wore a wide moustache thick as a cliché, and his round eyes sparkled darkly, knowing. He had his hands in the pockets of a cardigan that might have been passed down from his grandmother. He had not been undersold; his size notwithstanding, Fechner recognised the kind of presence that demanded attention. He was followed by a cat, a Bengal, a wild-looking creature with markings like a leopard. It moved around the room, staring at the new arrivals with measured indifference. Petrović greeted them warmly, shook their hands, then sat down in an armchair.

'That's Nefertiti,' he said, following their eyes. 'She is in charge. I am just her slave.' He laughed. 'Never trust anyone who does not trust an animal. They have something to hide.' He turned to Rusting. 'Do you have anything to hide?' The grin was gone, in its place a sober deadpan.

'Me? No,' Rusting said.

'No?' Petrović shook his head. He turned to Fechner. 'Is this true?'

Fechner felt his spine tingle. 'What man has nothing to hide?' he said.

Petrović smiled, nodded. 'This is a correct assessment.' His English was good, though the accent remained thick, clumsy. 'So, what can I do for you? What do you need?' He addressed the question to Fechner.

'Well,' said Rusting.

'Wait.' Petrović held a finger up. 'Who is in charge here?'

Rusting turned and looked at Fechner. Fechner spoke quickly. 'Robert is in charge.'

Petrović looked at them both, took them in.

Rusting continued. 'We want to expand. We have been importing from Bratislava.' He glanced towards Emil, who remained silent. 'But they don't have much, we need more. Electronics. Phones, TVs. And toys, trainers.'

'Toys? Like Buzz Lightyear? Or vibrators?'

Rusting smirked. 'I can sell both.'

'I hope to different people.' His humour, if it was humour, was dry.

Emil leaned forwards. He directed himself to Petrović. He spoke carefully, with evident respect. 'They are good customer. Every time, they pay. Never late.'

'You told me,' Petrović said. He turned to Rusting. 'So what, a lorry every month, every two months?'

Rusting looked to Fechner. 'Every two months maybe, to start?' Fechner nodded.

'Okay,' said Petrović.

'Okay?' Rusting looked at him now, cagey.

'Okay.'

'Can we see what you have? What about prices?'

Petrović turned to Fechner. 'Do you like my house?' he asked him. 'You have an eye, yes?' He nodded towards a credenza. 'What do you think?'

'It's nice,' Fechner said.

'Nice?'

'Danish?'

'Norway,' said Petrović. '1961. One sold last month for fifty thousand euros.'

'It's very nice,' Fechner repeated.

Petrović laughed. He turned back to Rusting. 'What is the phrase in English? Everything in the right place?'

'Everything in its right place,' Fechner said.

'Yes,' said Petrović. 'Everything in its right place. First dinner, then business. Maja is preparing dinner.'

They ate in a dining room at the rear of the house, where windows gave on to a garden, hidden from the street. Trees wept greenery on boisterous, flowering beds, rich in colour. Again, the room was tasteful, delicate, considered. The food was delicious, a leg of lamb roasted with garlic, lemon and herbs, falling easily off the bone. Potatoes had been soaked in the lamb juices then roasted separately. Fechner couldn't remember the last time he'd eaten so well. Petrović noticed his satisfaction.

'It's good, yes?'

'It's very good, yes,' Fechner agreed.

'You are a doctor.'

Fechner looked at him, careful now. He had not mentioned he was a doctor, not to Petrović nor even to Emil. He nodded.

Petrović smiled. 'You don't think I would do business without also doing research?'

Rusting shifted slightly in his comfortable chair.

'Why do you work like this if you are a doctor? Do you need money? Do you have big debt?'

'I don't have any debt,' Fechner said.

'So, you are greedy?'

136

Fechner smiled. 'Maybe I am greedy.'

Petrović swung himself around to face Rusting. 'And Mr Rusting was tried for killing his father.'

Emil's face was a blunder.

'You didn't know?' Petrović smiled at Emil. 'It's okay, he was not guilty.' He spoke again to Rusting. 'But it must have been strange for you? Sad? The accusation, on top of the grief.'

Rusting swallowed. A soft pink flush bloomed on his pale cheeks. 'Yes, it was,' he said.

'Did they ever catch the person who did it?' Petrović asked.

Rusting shook his head. 'No not yet.'

Petrović nodded. 'That is a shame. Closure is important.' The word was strange in his foreign mouth, deliberately impressive. He hemmed for a moment. 'Do you have closure?'

Rusting shrugged, politic.

Petrović lifted his fork, a chunk of lamb impaled, paused before his mouth. He pointed the meat first at Fechner, then at Rusting. 'And how do you know each other?'

Fechner felt like he had been dropped into the centre of a maze. He sensed Rusting's gaze heavy on him. 'I only met Robert a year ago,' he said eventually, 'a year and a half. In a bar in east Belfast. My father lives there. He wasn't well, and I was looking after him.' The story sounded thinner at such a remove.

Petrović nodded, finished chewing the piece of lamb. 'Your father lives in a bar?'

'He lives in east Belfast. Near the bar.' Fechner found a moment. 'He is the kind of man who leaves you needing a drink.'

Petrović raised his glass, took a mouthful of Romanian wine. He smiled and shook his head. 'So many fathers.'

The wine was finished, and another bottle opened. It was as good as the food had been, and Fechner had to stop himself drinking too quickly. Alert now, tentative, he watched Petrović. Petrović was loosening up, the drink effective, telling stories. He was funny, self-deprecating. Fechner noted though that with each deprecation he seemed to expand rather than diminish.

In a brief lull, as Petrović topped up his glass, Fechner asked him, 'Did you always do this?'

'This?' Petrović was confused.

'Your work, your business.'

'Let me tell you something,' Petrović said. 'I grew up in a tiny village, not even a village, eighty kilometres from Belgrade, in the south. It was poor, like somewhere from two hundred years ago. No roads, no concrete roads I mean, just dirt. Dirt tracks. My father, my mother, seven children. I am the youngest. I know, you did not think that, the youngest, I do not seem like the youngest, everyone says that. Tiny, scrawny you say in English. Someone saw a photograph of me later and told me that word, a woman. Scrawny, she said, pointing at me and laughing. But she was correct, she was very correct, I was. My father farmed a small piece of land. He planted it for potatoes, like Ireland.' He laughed, but he wasn't smiling. 'That's what we would eat, potatoes. Other things too, but mostly potatoes, and cabbage of course. We had some meat we traded for that we kept in a smokehouse, to make it last as long as possible. But we were always hungry. Nine people, and enough food for five maybe. He was a bad farmer, my father, but he was an even worse gambler. He lost our mule in a game of cards. We had some family who lived near and tried to help, but he was too proud, too stupid. He went out and ploughed the fields himself, put the harness for the mule on his own back and walked up and down the fields for four days until he fell over and died. His heart—' He paused, took a drink, seemed to consider.

'I am sorry,' Fechner said.

'You are sorry, I am sorry. It doesn't matter. We went to bury him, all of us. The cemetery, is that the right word?' – he waited for Fechner's nod of confirmation – 'The cemetery was ten miles away, in the village where he was born, where his family was from. We put on all our best clothes, which were not very good, and we buried him, and when we came back someone had went in to our smokehouse and stole all the meat. Stolen. Stolen all the meat.' He let the silence sit there. He seemed to be experiencing it again himself, the return, the disappointment, the bitterness.

'And the strange thing, we knew who did it. It was a man who was a friend of my father. A friend. Can you believe. So my mother, God rest her soul, she said we must do nothing, say nothing, that there are people who must suffer, and God is the only judge. We moved the next day to my father's village. We lived with his family. They split us up because there were too many of us, we went to different relatives. Two of my sisters, they were nearly sixteen already, sixteen years old I mean, they went to Belgrade, to work. My brother, Stefan, he died too the next year when a tractor fell over on a hill on top of him. Anyway, all of this I am saying because I decided then, when I was nine years old, that one day I will have money and food and a house and good things. I just decided. I would not live like my father, I would be different. I was not greedy, I just decided. When I was twenty-four, I came back from Tirana, where I was working for a man who smuggled cigarettes and dogs, yes cigarettes and dogs, puppies. And I went back to the village, the house I mean that we used to live in, just to see it. And the man, the friend of my father

139

who had stolen our food, he was living in it. And I killed him. I strangled him. I have never killed anyone else, I do not do that, I am not that kind of person. I am just telling you because, well, because you asked how I am here. That is what happened. I took all the money he had in his house, which was a surprising large amount, things seemed to be very different for him then, and I took the money and went to Belgrade and started to smuggle cigarettes and then other things. And now. Well, now I am here.'

He looked around the room with impassive satisfaction. He saw Fechner's eye on him, Fechner's expression, neither hot nor cold. Maybe he misread him, Petrović; maybe he thought Fechner was judging him.

'A few years ago, someone asked me, do you enjoy it?' He stared at Fechner, at Rusting. '"Do you enjoy it?" he asked me. All of this he meant,' his hand described a circle, taking in the food, the wine, the room, the house, the life he had built, the world he had created, 'and I said: "That is not the point."' He stared hard at Fechner. 'Do you understand? I said to him: "That is not the point."'

After dinner they threw numbers together. It was less a negotiation, more Petrović explaining how he worked. The legal provenance of the goods was his concern, and he could provide paperwork and transport so that by the time they arrived in Ireland they would be clean. He could get them as far as Dún Laoghaire, but the journey north to Belfast was their responsibility. He took them through recent lists of what he had had available. He agreed to take them, when they returned from their meeting the following day in Novi Sad, to one of his current warehouses, though he had little to show them. He didn't store goods, he said, he moved them.

It was almost eleven when they prepared to leave. Fechner used the bathroom, and on his way back through the hallway, Maja appeared.

'Mladen would like to speak with you,' she said.

Fechner felt his chest contract, the cower on him. He nodded, for fear his voice might betray him. She led him through a sitting room into an office, where Petrović stood waiting. She left them, closing the door gently behind.

'Forgive me,' Petrović said. 'I just need to know who I am dealing with. Emil recommends you, and I trust him. But I am a careful man, you understand.'

He paused. Fechner wondered if he was supposed to say something.

'I understand. Is there something you need to know?'

'I have just a feeling,' Petrović said. 'A hesitation. Your friend Robert, he does not say much. But he seethes. I do not need, what is the saying, a loose cannon.'

Fechner shook his head.

'Here we call them time bombs.' Petrović smiled. 'Boom! You know?' He pointed at Fechner.

'He is not a loose cannon.' Fechner's heart struck with faithful violence, pounding out his commitment. He felt his voice weaken though. 'He is not a time bomb. He is reliable.'

'He is not weak? I see he is a big man, but his eyes are soft. You believe in him?'

Fechner shook his head, resisted. Resisted Petrović, resisted too his own sick vision, his own dismay.

'You misunderstand him. He is quiet tonight, yes. He is not used to leaving Ireland, leaving Belfast. But on his streets, what he says goes.'

'What he says goes? What does this mean?'

'What he says will happen, happens.'

141

'And what does he say will happen?'

Fechner floundered. 'Look, if you do not want to work with us you do not have to.'

Petrović smiled, reached out and touched Fechner's shoulder gently, familiarly. 'It's okay,' he said. 'It's just business.' He walked to the door, opened it for Fechner to pass. He followed. 'In the other room,' he said to Fechner, 'Maja is asking him the same questions about you.'

As she had promised, the hotel manager found them an extra room. Fechner gathered up his belongings, threw them carelessly into his suitcase.

'What do you think?' Rusting, sitting on his bed, asked him.

'About what?'

'About the offer. Your man Petrović.'

'The numbers seem good. If he can deliver what he says, we would do well enough.'

Rusting was silent.

'What do you think?' Fechner said.

'Would you trust him all right? He seems like he's a hand in every pocket. Nosy bastard isn't he.'

'We've nothing to hide.'

'No, I know.'

Rusting's eyes looked sore, tired. He blanched, grimaced, suppressing a yawn. He was suddenly, sitting before Fechner, just a boy, six, seven years old, insecure, needy, feeble. Flesh from flesh, muscle from muscle, the attrition of years unwound, undone, and with each layer excised, power excised also, his vital strength evaporated. How far back do you have to go to get to the emptiness, the clean slate? No clean slate though; even the glint in the eye has purpose. Who arrives unspoiled, really? Who would want

142

to? Without guile, how could make anything of the world, of yourself? No tree without the breaking of soil. What would you be, thought Fechner, but a version of your father, your mother?

The following morning, Ivo drove them to Novi Sad. Emil's contact met them in a hotel in Petrovaradin, a modern, glassy affair with all the character of a McDonald's. Over breakfast, Borko Marić – a white South African with an accent to match – boasted of what he could do for them, the influence and contacts he had, not only in Serbia but also in Romania and Bulgaria, as far east even as Ukraine. He spoke quickly, aggressively, without pauses, his words railway carriages coupled together taking you somewhere whether you wanted to go or not. Rusting simpered, easily won over by the swank, the bluster. Maybe too by Marić's manner: pally, gangster lite, dripping with cheap menace. *Very Rusting*, Fechner thought bitterly. Rusting's dumb face – Fechner couldn't stop noticing, try as he might – seeking approval. Immediately, effortlessly, Fechner hated Marić. Hated him for his crassness, for his grubby love of money, for the way he tried to pretend they were all friends, all *the same kind of people*. Worse, though: he hated him for what he brought out in Rusting. He showed him a stooge, a sucker, persuaded by cheap performance, by bombast.

After breakfast, Marić took them to a warehouse in the west of the city, across the Danube. It was well enough stocked, mostly with Chinese-made electronics, TVs, laptops and the like. A decent selection, but nothing to die for, all said. Still, Rusting mugged for him, pattered after him, receptive to the oversell. Fechner bit his tongue at the end as Rusting promised a quick answer once the trip was complete.

143

They returned to Subotica. The journey back was subdued, the discord silent but palpable. Emil enjoyed sentimental traditional music, which he played loudly on the stereo, limning the mood comic. Back at the hotel, they nursed bitter coffees and talked through the pros and cons of both offers, both opportunities. Fechner feigned circumspect, as deferential to Rusting as a tailor. But there was a sharpness just below the surface, a misgiving, and Fechner knew he must be careful. Rusting was not smart enough to see it, but Fechner felt it bright in himself, in the way he answered back a little too quickly, too robustly. He tried to ignore what else he knew now of Rusting, what he *felt*, but the weakness would not be denied. Still he was patient; he knew he could make his words wrap around their target, place his idea into the mouth of Rusting, so that it was he, in the end, who made the suggestion that they should go with Petrović. Fechner nodded and sagely agreed.

Petrović's inventory, as he had warned, was minimal, but Fechner was nonetheless impressed. He showed them the transport depot, took them through logs of items, showed them where he shipped to and how often. Everything notated but all on computer, encrypted, not a scrap of paper in sight. At the very least, if they did a deal here, there'd be some confidence in the operation. After the survey, Petrović took them to meet a 'friend'. He lifted his hands from the wheel to draw the commas in the air. Like a business partner, he said, but instead of money, she brings wisdom and guidance.

'Guidance?' Fechner asked.

'Spiritual guidance,' said Petrović.

Fechner caught his eye in the mirror, but Petrović played unironic.

Ksenija – Senka for short – ran a teahouse, a modest little

unit in a run of characterless buildings downtown, close to the synagogue. It was closed, being after seven on a Sunday evening, but Petrović called her, and within a minute she was unlocking the door and ushering them inside.

She was dark-haired, slight. Hard to put a number on her, but at least as old as Petrović. Her eyes had astonishing clarity, her gaze – brazenly thrown upon them, top to bottom – seemed to Fechner gnostic. She greeted Petrović in Serbian, led them into the rear of the building, into a small kitchen, directed them to sit down. She began to make tea, stirring a handful of leaves into a pot.

They drank, the tea bitter but refreshing. She spoke with Petrović, ignoring the foreigners. Their voices were soft, familiar. Fechner recognised trust, affection; he wondered at their relation. She was sexless, but she had a strange, compelling urgency, a draw. Petrović's shoulders tightened as he leaned towards her, supplicant. Fechner felt Rusting's glare on him, asking with his eyes what they were doing there. Fechner ignored him.

After a few minutes, their tea finished, Senka leaned across and snatched Fechner's cup. She upturned it on to a saucer, a sly smile creeping on to her face.

'I asked her to read your leaves,' Petrović said.

She lifted the cup in one hand, turned it over from the right, set it into the palm of the other. Fechner watched her face as she stared down into it. For ten, fifteen seconds she sat there, silent. Then she glanced up at him, a crafty gleam brilliant on her.

'Pretrpeli ste gubitak,' she said.

Fechner looked to Petrović. 'She says you have suffered a loss,' he said.

A sneer, impulsive, caught Fechner's face. 'Yes my wife left me,' he said. 'Last year.'

145

Petrović translated.

She shook her head, quickly. 'Ne, ne.' She stuck a bony finger out, towards his chest. 'Dublje.'

'Deeper.' Petrović smiled.

Fechner's face corrected. Against his will, she had his attention.

'Uvek je bilo tu,' she said, looking directly at him. 'Uvek je bilo tu, zar ne?'

Petrović spoke slowly. 'It was always there, no?'

A softness caught at Fechner's throat. He tried to laugh it off, but it came out not as laughter but as a low squawk. Fechner didn't believe in this woman but some part of him wanted to.

'Everyone has loss,' he said. 'So what.'

Petrović translated. Senka smiled.

'Želiš nešto. Šta hoćeš?'

'You want something, she says.' Petrović was sober. 'What do you want?'

'We want a good deal, a good supplier.' Fechner nodded.

Petrović conveyed.

'Ne, ne.' Her voice sharpened. 'Tebe nije briga za novac! Šta hoćeš?'

'She says you don't care about money.'

Impulsive, Fechner's eyes shot to Rusting. He saw her mark it, felt himself in error. He had the insane impression that she was stealing from him. A dull, clammy panic seized him.

'This is nonsense.' Rusting spoke, suddenly. His big eyes mocked, indulgent. 'No offence,' he said, lifting his palms up. 'I'm just saying.'

Senka turned her face to him. Back and forth then she cast her eyes, Rusting to Fechner to Rusting, seeking some clarity. She reached across and took Rusting's cup, performed

146

the same slow ritual – the emptying, the turn, the shift from one hand to the other. Her gaze sober then upon the leaves. Fechner could see them, tiny marks spread around the surface like scattered stars.

'I don't believe in this,' Rusting said.

'Ti si veliki čovek.'

'You are a big man,' Petrović translated.

Rusting laughed.

'Ali iznutra se osećaš malim.'

Petrović paused. Rusting looked to him, something dull and hesitant passing across his face.

'But inside you feel small,' he said.

A keen thrill ran through Fechner. He watched Rusting's demeanour, casual, give to caution.

'Vi ste nedodirljivi', she reached across the table and tried to take his hand, but he snatched it back. 'Ali želiš da te dodiruju.'

Rusting stared at Petrović, waiting. Petrović coy, cunning. 'She said you are untouchable,' he said. He paused. 'But you want to be touched.'

'You don't know me,' Rusting said.

Petrović translated. Senka smiled. She leaned forward into Rusting's space. She reached out her hand, drew a circle in the air, encompassed him. 'Lavu je lakše da veruje da je Bog na njegovoj strani nego na strani jedne gazele.'

'Look, what are we doing here?' Rusting said to Petrović. 'Is this part of the deal, or what?'

Petrović looked at Senka. Her eyes sparkled with triumph, or pleasure, or cruelty.

'Okay, let us go,' he said.

He dropped them back at the hotel. They shook hands. He promised he would contact them during the week to begin arrangements. Fechner lingered as Rusting stepped inside.

147

'What did she say at the end?' he asked.

Petrović shook his head. 'It doesn't matter.'

'What did she say?' Fechner insisted.

Petrović smiled. 'It's an old saying. The lion finds it more easy to believe God is on his side than the side of the gazelle.'

Fechner and Rusting had a drink in the lobby. Fechner was dour, chary. He pleaded tiredness. It was ten o'clock already. They would leave for Belgrade early the next morning to catch their flight. They said goodnight, went each to their room. While packing, Fechner couldn't find his passport. Perhaps he'd left it in Rusting's room. He walked down the corridor, knocked gently on his door. There was no response. He rapped a little harder, listened for movement. Nothing shifted. He didn't want to wake him, but he felt now an urgency. He made his way downstairs to the reception, asked if anyone had handed it in.

The young assistant rifled around the desk. 'I can't see,' he said. 'There is no note.'

'It's okay,' Fechner apologised. 'I'm sure it's in my friend's room.'

'I will ask him when he comes back,' said the receptionist.

'It's okay, he's sleeping,' Fechner said.

'No, no, he went out. A few minutes ago.'

Fechner shook his head. 'He went out?'

'Yes, just maybe five minutes.'

'Did he say where he was going?'

'No.' The young man was cautious now.

Fechner walked out into the courtyard in front of the hotel. The air snatched at his neck, cool after the warmth of the day. On an impulse, he walked in the direction of the centre, the bars they'd passed the day before. He did not expect to find Rusting. He decided not to care. He had a beer in one bar, a touristy spot with a courtyard out the back and a woman singing folk songs. Her voice was plain, but Fechner was bent on the sentimental. He moved on, walking aimlessly. On a street near the railway station, he saw a group of young people smoking outside a night-club, Ivo among them. He was smoking quickly, anxiously. Fechner raised his hand, and Ivo spotted him. Fechner caught the hesitation on his face, the inclination to walk off. But he checked himself, waved back. Fechner crossed the street.

'You too?' Ivo said.

Fechner didn't know what he meant. 'Me too?' He gambled. 'Yes, me too.'

'Why did you not come at the same time?'

'I told him I wasn't coming. But I changed my mind.'

Ivo shrugged. 'Okay, let us go.'

Fechner followed him. Ivo lit another cigarette, dragged silently. He didn't look at Fechner. He ducked left, down a side street, then another, then right into an alleyway. Halfway along, he stopped before an unmarked steel door. He rang a bell that was hidden behind a blind brick. The door swung open, and a huge bearded bull of a man stepped out. Ivo nodded at Fechner, and the beard stared at him, assessing. He jerked his head, ushered him inside.

'Thank you,' Fechner said.

Ivo looked at him and laughed.

Fechner followed the man along a corridor at the end of which was a makeshift bar. A couple of shelves of liquor, a fridge filled with cheap beer and vodka. A few tables, at which sat a handful of men, who stared at him like he was a cowboy entering a saloon. Fechner knew where he was all right.

'A drink?' the beard asked him, in English.

Fechner shook his head. 'My friend,' he said. 'Where is he?'

'You want to join?'

'Yes,' Fechner said. It was hot, clammy. He could smell the sweat. He ignored the flat, hungry eyes of the other men. Noises, unspecific, reached them from unseen rooms. The beard took him along another corridor, showed him a door. Fechner hesitated, feeling the anger turn in him, the resentment. He'd found a line, but he didn't need to cross it, he could still walk away. His throat was dry, but a savage need gripped him. He stuck his hand out, pushed the door open and stepped inside.

The door shut silently behind him. The room was dark, save for a sickly blue light thrown from a couple of bulbs attached to the rear wall. There was Rusting, facing the wall, away from Fechner. He was on his knees, arms outstretched, like you would prostrate yourself before an altar, or a god. He was topless. Above him stood a rake of a man, lank, gaunt, dressed in jeans and a T-shirt. He had thick, black, wiry hair, uneven stubble. In the dank teal light, he looked ill. A cigarette hung limp in his mouth. In one hand, he held some kind of lash, and in the other the end of a chain that Fechner realised was around Rusting's neck. The lash realised someone had walked in, and looked up. Fechner stared at him, silent. In the pause, Rusting sensed something. He went to move, to turn and see, but the man took his boot and pressed it against Rusting's face, prevented him.

'Ostati,' he hissed. 'Ostati, kućko.'

Rusting stayed.

The man took a drag on the cigarette, threw Fechner a little grin. His eyes sang with appetite. Then he lifted the lash and threw it heavy on to Rusting's back. The sound

150

rang out clean, echoed flat off the dead walls. Rusting's back arced up. He gasped. Fechner couldn't see his face, but he could imagine it.

'Da? Ili ne?' the man said.

'Da,' Rusting said.

'Da?'

'Da, da.'

The lash came down heavy again, and again Rusting's skin sang sharp, raw. Fechner stared. The man took a rough toke, caught it wrong. He coughed, brutal. His sick lungs hissed. Fechner turned and quickly pulled open the door. He strode fast along the corridor, through the bar and out to the exit. The doorman stared at him but leaned down and unlocked it. Fechner pushed out into the street.

He was sweating. He felt the air stinging now, cold. The alley was deserted. He shivered, pulled tight on his collar, walked towards the hotel, turned, walked back. He stood before the steel door again, shuffling, equivocating. He closed his eyes and saw Rusting, restored, imperious, emerging resplendent, like a warrior. But the door stayed shut, mocking him.

Fortunately, Monday was Ivo's day off. Emil drove them to the airport himself. Rusting snoozed against the window in the back seat. Fechner sat up front.

'You are happy then?' Emil asked him.

'Happy?'

'You got what you came for?'

Fechner nodded. 'Yes, thank you.'

Emil was no fool, but the sombre mood was not his prison. He glanced in the mirror.

'Rusting,' he said. 'Is he sick? Or only tired?'

Fechner turned his head, looked at Rusting's face, artless,

151

trusting to dreams. His head bobbed easy to the movement of the car. His mouth hung half open, like a child's awaiting a spoon. 'Both I think,' said Fechner.

11

Fechner once asked Abraham if he believed in the soul.

'In 1901, in Dorchester, Massachusetts,' Abraham told the boy, 'Dr Duncan MacDougall actually weighed the human soul. He had a set of scales specially constructed, on which he placed a patient, selected for his proximity to death. In the company of four witnesses – also medical doctors – he kept the scales balanced as the man's breath dwindled. When the patient died, something extraordinary occurred. *Suddenly, coincident with death,* McDougall wrote, *the beam end dropped with an audible stroke hitting against the lower limiting bar and remaining there with no rebound. The loss was ascertained to be three-fourths of an ounce.*

'In the months that followed,' Abraham continued, 'he repeated the experiment with five other patients, four men and a woman. In every case bar one, their bodies, on death, immediately lost a fraction of their weight. In the one outstanding case, of a lethargic, heavy man, the weight drop did not occur immediately, but after about a minute. *I believe that in this case,* MacDougall declared, *that of a phlegmatic man slow of thought and action, that the soul remained suspended in the body after death, during the minute that elapsed before its freedom. There is no other way of accounting*

153

for it, and it is what might be expected to happen in a man of the subject's temperament.

'When he later carried out a similar experiment with fifteen dogs, he found no change in weight upon death. This confirmed his suspicion that only humans have souls.

'I believe that the soul,' Abraham told his nephew, 'is an accretion. You understand an accretion?'

Young Fechner shook his head.

'An accretion is when something builds up. Layer upon layer upon layer. Each thought you think, each longing you have, each kindness you perform, or crime – layer upon layer it grows. Of course, I know what you're thinking. Any one of these things in isolation is nothing. What is a thought? It is not real, it has no presence. You cannot reach out and touch a thought, a feeling. That is what you are thinking, is it not? Well, that is true enough. But thoughts and feelings take up residence inside you, and invisibly, imperceptibly, they grow and grow. They *become* your soul. When you are sad and feel a lump in your throat,' Abraham said, 'that is your soul getting caught. When you are scared, and you feel, in the pit of your stomach, something tighten, that is your soul. When a rage comes on you, and you feel hot, that is your soul. Each time growing, expanding. When you are young, like you are, your soul is small. But when you are old, like me, then your soul will be large. It will fill you. Sometimes you will forget about it – many people forget about theirs for a very long time – but sooner or later you will remember, you will sense it again inside you, occupying you. Demanding something of you. Never fail to listen.'

Fechner stared at his uncle in frank, wary scepticism. He knew already, of course he did, the power of his own hatred, his own fear. Even, perhaps, in moments with Abraham, his own love. But he had thought, if he had thought at all, that it would wash off him, that a time would come when he would shake himself loose into the world and make himself up anew, present himself as he wanted to be seen, as he wanted to *be*.

He shook his head at Abraham. 'No,' he said.

'No?'

Fechner again shook his head.

'Well, you must be a different kind of man than me then,' Abraham said.

Fechner began to account for twenty-one grams. Half a golf ball. One suit in a deck of cards. Five dice. Four sheets of foolscap paper. A small mouse. It was, he supposed, after all, not so very heavy. Still it became, as these things do in childhood, an obsession. Each time a thought occurred to him, a feeling he caught himself aware of, he would wonder how it shaped his soul, what kind of mark it left. Not only feelings. Hatreds, desires. His mother was sick now, and he could not sever the love from the frustration, the disappointment, the betrayal. Guilt too, of course. He should not have weighed the mouse. He began to think he had a creature inside, eating whatever Fechner gave him. And try as he did to resist, Fechner gave him plenty.

A few days after they returned, Fechner was in his office, scheduling surgeries. The secretary stuck her head round the door.

'There's two people here to see you,' she said.

'Marie, I'm busy,' Fechner said.

'I told them, but they're insistent.' The annoyance bristled on her. 'Why don't you tell them yourself.'

'Who is it?'

'A couple of youths.' She said the word like it might contaminate her. 'They say they know you.'

'All right,' he said. 'Send them in.'

A minute later she returned trailing them behind her. Fechner felt her beady eyes on him. 'Is there anything I can get for you all?' she said.

He turned to Kenner and Polio. 'Do youse want a cup of tea?'

Tight-lipped, Kenner shook his head.

'No,' said Polio.

'We're all right, thank you Marie,' Fechner said, and closed the door behind her.

'Well what a lovely surprise.'

'You weren't answering your phone.' Kenner's tone was sharp.

'How are you, Paul?' Fechner said. 'Haven't seen you in a while.'

'Manny wants to come back,' said Kenner. 'But he wants some assurance that Rusting will leave him alone. Can you do something?'

'Would you like to sit down?' Fechner said.

'Can you do something?' Kenner repeated.

'What would you like me to do?'

'Speak to Rusting. He listens to you, doesn't he?'

'Does he?'

Kenner was looking around the room. He seemed to have expected something more impressive.

'Where's McManus now?' Fechner said.

'He's still in London, but he hates it. He doesn't know anybody. He went to some cousin of his ma's, but he's an asshole. He just wants to come home.'

'To do what?'

'Does it matter?' Kenner had conviction.

'What do you think, Paul?'

Long out of pills by now, he had to fight to keep the

shakes at bay. He spoke quietly. 'I think he should be able to come home if he wants to come home.'

'All right,' said Fechner. 'I'll have a word. But I can't make any promises.'

'I didn't ask you to make promises,' said Kenner.

'Okay. Well I have work to do here.'

Kenner opened the door. 'Just do something,' he said.

Fechner went to the White Star Line on Saturday evening, around eight. Rusting was there already, holding court, a crowd of onlookers gawping on his tales. Marić – the gangster they'd met in Novi Sad – had become in his telling Borko the fool, the clown, Rusting's fawning admiration revised into mockery. He worked the South African accent clumsy in his mouth, laid on Soprano thick. Fechner listened without interrupting, answered the glances thrown questioning at him with a wry smile. Rusting was glazed already, three or four pints in.

One of the regulars turned to Fechner. 'Some trip then by the sounds of it?'

The image of Rusting prostrate on the floor, chain around his neck, the lash catching his raw back, leapt into Fechner's mind.

'It was,' he said.

'What was your man like?' Rusting said, drawing Fechner in. 'A nutcase, eh, wasn't he?'

'I'm going to get a drink here,' Fechner said. 'Anyone want one?'

Fechner sipped lethargic, two pints in two hours, observed Rusting charm and flatter. He was well versed by now; he knew Rusting's manners, knew the turns, the shifts, from humility to demand, boredom to insistence. He recognised the small movements that announced the

157

change in temper, in patience. What kind of gift was it to have such a threat that others will sacrifice their own desire to see you satisfied?

By eleven, Fechner had had enough. He slipped out quietly. He was about to get into a taxi when he heard his name.

'James.' Rusting had followed him out. 'You're not leaving already?'

'Early start tomorrow,' Fechner said.

'You heard anything yet from Petrović?' Rusting said.

'Not yet, no.'

'Are you coming here or not?' the taxi driver said.

Rusting leaned over. 'He's not,' he said, and shut the door.

Rusting walked around the back of the bar to the beer garden. Resentful, Fechner followed. It was empty save for a few young lads in one corner sharing a spliff, who ignored them. They sat at a table opposite each other.

'I'm worried,' Rusting said. 'What if he doesn't come through?'

'Why would he not come through?' Fechner said.

'When did he say he'd contact us?'

'He said he'd have a list for us this week.' Fechner was short.

'But he didn't.'

'He didn't.'

'What's going on with you?'

Fechner weighed it up. Rusting was half drunk. He looked around, made sure they were not being observed.

'McManus would like to come home.'

Rusting stiffened. His head cocked to one side, careful. Fechner watched the arms tend inwards.

'He would like an assurance that it's okay.'

'What's that supposed to mean? Assurance from who?' said Rusting.

158

'From you.'

'Why wouldn't it be okay?' Rusting wore his agitation badly. Fechner saw the body fight the alcohol, felt the wild attempt to get on top of something. Too late.

'Look,' said Fechner. 'I know what was going on.'

Rusting stared at him. For the first time since he had encountered him, Fechner saw fear, or something very like it. An enormous swell of sympathy happened in Fechner, instinctual.

'What do you know?'

'It doesn't matter,' Fechner said. 'He just wants to know it won't keep going. You won't make him keep doing it, I mean.'

Rusting rocked slightly, back and forth. Fechner looked away, embarrassed.

'Does anybody else know?' Rusting said, eventually.

'No,' Fechner said.

'You didn't tell anybody?'

'I didn't tell anybody.'

Rusting's face teetered.

'So, you are telling me he can come back? You understand what I'm asking?'

Rusting nodded. 'Yes. It's not what you think.'

'You don't need to explain anything to me,' Fechner said. He could hear himself as he said it, taste the revulsion. Rusting looked at him with big, open eyes, gratitude heavy in them. It made it worse. Rusting leaned over and put his hand on top of Fechner's.

'Thank you,' Rusting said. 'Thank you for understanding. I knew of all people you would.' He looked so tender, so weak. His wet eyes sparkled.

'It's all right,' said Fechner, looking away, disgusted.

By the following weekend there was still no word from

159

the Serbs. Fechner was certain now that Ivo had tattled to Rusting's proclivity – not just Rusting's, in Ivo's eyes – and Emil would have informed Petrović. Petrović, surely, had decided it wasn't worth it. Too much scruple, too much *boom*. It had to have crossed Rusting's mind by now that his indiscretion had wrecked the arrangement. But he hadn't come clean to Fechner about it, and nor had Fechner told him what he'd seen. A brittle, glowing silence now held. Fechner felt Rusting careful around him, fussy. He deferred to Fechner now, and Fechner could sense it, a strange redistribution – of will, or jurisdiction, or licence – beginning to take shape. It unnerved Fechner, upset the balance, the clarity of his own devotion, his own *motive*.

On the first Friday in June he met Buchanan for a meal in a new Japanese restaurant on the Lisburn Road. Buchanan probed, expressed his old concern.

'Some have remarked that you are not yourself lately,' Buchanan said.

'Thank you,' said Fechner.

'You know what I mean. What's this trip I hear you took?'

'The sushi is good isn't it?' Fechner said.

'I heard it was with some entrepreneur who deals in laptops. Are you short of money or something?'

'Do I ask you every detail of your life, Charles?' he said.

Buchanan threw his hands up in mock surrender.

The main arrived, a fish curry to share. They battered through, found some of their old pleasure, their old ease. They were contemplating dessert when Fechner's phone buzzed. He stared at the unknown number.

'Sorry, Charles,' he picked it up. 'Hello, James Fechner here.'

'It's Camile, sorry.'

'Who?' Fechner threw Buchanan a face.

'Camile. From the bar. The White Star Line. It's just, I think you might need to come down here. It's your father.'

Fechner stood up, waved an apologetic finger, walked outside.

'What do you mean it's my father?'

'There's some old lad here. He says he's your father,' said Camile. 'He's had a few drinks now, he's fairly hammered. He's mouthing off, telling stories. I just think it might be better if you came and got him.'

'What kind of stories?'

'Well not good ones, put it that way. He's not exactly being complimentary about you.'

He could taste the sushi repeating.

'All right I'll be there.'

He went back inside.

'Everything okay?' Buchanan asked.

'My father's had a turn,' said Fechner. He threw some notes on the table. 'I need to go, I'm sorry.'

Fechner drove quickly across the city. He pushed into the bar. Sure enough, there in the corner beside the slots, his father in drunken brio. When he saw his son, his eyes narrowed with delight and malice.

'Behold the man!' Edward said. He tried to stand up but wobbled. One of the regulars standing nearby caught him, steadied him. 'That there is my son,' Edward said. 'A big man round here now apparently.' He stuttered with the drink but the effect was not missed. 'I could tell you things though.'

Fechner walked firmly to him, took his arm. 'Let's get you home shall we,' he said.

Edward snatched his arm away. 'I'm not going home.'

Fechner burned with embarrassment, but the rage was stronger.

'You are, actually.' He grabbed his arm again. This time, he was not shrugged off. The regular caught Fechner's eye, took the other arm. Edward turned to him, nearly fell again. Between them the two men held him up and steered him to the door. They got him into Fechner's car.

'You'll be all right?' the man said to Fechner.

'Thank you,' Fechner said.

His father said nothing. Fechner drove quickly, sullen, chasing thoughts. At his father's house, he dragged him out of the car, hustled him inside. Edward scowled, his face full of drink and enmity.

'You're no better than me,' he slurred.

Fechner shunted his father into an armchair. 'Shut up. What is wrong with you?'

Fechner stood over him. Edward laughed. Decades of contempt shaped his face ugly. Edward's eyes were tiny holes. Fechner saw himself in them, shivered. He felt the future tighten around him. A thousand years of this were coming, he knew. A million.

His phone rang. He lifted it from his pocket, saw Rusting's name illuminated. He hesitated. He felt Edward's glare on him. He punched the screen, turned away into the kitchen and out into the back yard.

'Hello,' he said.

'Are you all right?' Rusting, concerned.

'What do you mean?'

'I heard your da was down in the Star causing a scene.'

Fechner breathed deeply. 'Yeah, I just brought him back.'

'What was that about?'

'I don't know. Fucking fathers.'

Rusting hung on in silence.

'Look,' he said, eventually. 'I'm at the gym, come on round when you're done. I know where Preston keeps his whisky.'

He waited until Edward was asleep, then walked the fifteen minutes through Victoria Park. It was dark now, quiet after eleven, the summer sky deepening purple to black. In the silence of birds, the park was pacific. Trees loomed above in their slumber, like giants. Not a soul disturbed him. *It is good*, he remembered, *for man to be alone.* He wondered if he had that right.

The gym was in darkness. The door was unlocked though, and he stepped inside cautiously. At the rear a small light was on in Blair's office. He moved towards it. He felt his heart thump, faster, keener. Carefully, he nudged the door open. The room was empty, a bottle of whisky lonely on Blair's desk. He stood and listened. He heard nothing save his own lungs. He retreated, moved down the corridor towards the weights room. He pushed the door open. There was Rusting, sitting on one of the benches. He looked up at Fechner. He wore only tracksuit bottoms. His huge frame glistened.

Fechner hesitated. 'Sorry,' he said. 'I didn't realise you were actually working out.'

'I was,' Rusting said. 'Come on in.'

Fechner stepped into the room. The smell of sweat hung in the air, damp.

'Some night for you then eh?' Rusting said.

'Yeah,' said Fechner. 'I don't know what's wrong with him.'

'Sure he's always been like that though has he not?'

Fechner nodded. The silence hung thick between them.

'I'd say what you need,' Rusting said, 'is to take out some aggression.'

163

He turned around, lifted a bamboo rod from the ground behind him.

Fechner stared, blinked.

'It will help, James. Believe me. I seen it in you. You want to. I want you to.'

'No.'

'You do. I seen it in you. You think you hide it but you don't.'

'You're wrong.'

Rusting fixed him. 'No, I'm not. I know you, James. I know who you are. I seen it from the beginning. I seen the hunger on you.'

He handed Fechner the cane. Fechner found himself taking it.

Rusting turned and made his way slowly down on to his knees. He put his arms on the floor and set his forehead on them. Fechner stared at his back, the thin lines almost faded. He felt the rod heavy in his palm, a nervous vitality pulsing quicker, stronger. He tried to speak, but his mouth was empty.

'Go on,' he heard Rusting say.

He refused, but he felt his grip tighten. His hand, against all his will, against his instruction, moved into the air, raising the stick.

'Go on,' Rusting said again. 'Go on James.'

The first blow was weak, a tiny smack.

'Come on,' Rusting said. 'Do it properly. Hurt me.'

Fechner saw another blow fall, a little harder this time. He saw Rusting feel it, saw his back arch. The sound caught thicker, carried a little of Rusting's pain.

'That's it,' Rusting said. 'Come on James. Come on.'

Another blow, harder again. Rusting gasped. He went to say something, but Fechner had the rhythm now, drew the arm back and threw it down again, harder. Dark red marks blossomed on Rusting's back. Another blow, and another, and Fechner saw the skin open. The line of blood persuaded. Fechner followed himself in disbelief, again and again. He does nothing, and yet here is Rusting, floundering now below him, his body jerking, rising and falling at Fechner's discretion.

'All right,' Rusting said, but Fechner ignored him. He heard only the pulse of his own blood, hammering hammering hammering, rushing furiously through him. Down the rod went, again. A real cry of pain then, from Rusting, a moan, but again, quickly, up and down. Rusting tried to raise his head, but it caught him across the shoulder blades, opened another line, drove him back into the floor. Faster now, stronger, and Rusting saying something, *enough* maybe, or *stop*, or *Fechner*, and then he wasn't saying anything. His body jerked, convulsed, given over now to its own language. Fechner went on. Like a dream it was, an entrancement, Fechner nothing but movement, punishment. Suddenly, he caught himself. He saw Rusting lying on the ground below him, his back raw, gashed up, blood pleading. He stopped. His senses, briefly intertwined into one blurred rush, one pure, unfettered flow, began to extricate themselves, reannounce their presence. Only the tiny heave of Rusting's back gave any sign of life. Fechner stared, at first in shock but then, impulsive, in concern, in *recognition*. He dropped the stick, fell to his knees, put his arms around Rusting, gently, carefully lifted him. He turned Rusting's face towards him. 'Robert,' he said. 'Robert.' Rusting's eyes were closed. His blood reddened Fechner's shirt. 'Robert, come on.' There was urgency in Fechner's voice now. He put his hand on Rusting's neck. Gently, he turned him round, cradled him. 'Come on Robert,' he said again, his hand on Rusting's wet face. Rusting groaned. He blinked his eyes open, and looked up at Fechner. In his eyes was something that might have been fear but Fechner knew wasn't fear. 'Look,' Fechner said. 'You're all right. You're all right now. That's enough.'

12

The doctors' summer shindig was in late August, in a repurposed barn outside Lisburn. The old made new, newer. A pig roasted on a spit, cava flowed like water. A string quartet pivoted from Mozart to Kanye, to murmured delight. Buchanan had urged his friend to show his face, though in the end it wasn't Buchanan's invite, but Katherine's, that he accepted.

He had seen her again a couple of times already, once for a meal at The Muddlers Club, and once for a walk up at Redburn, where they'd spent many afternoons in the early days finding their humour with one another. He was surprised how easily some of the old comfort returned, though he hesitated to trust it. There was a recalibration though, a new measure. They were careful with each other; slower to speak, quicker to listen. Katherine had changed too; not chastened but pacified, a subtle acceptance evident in the way she carried herself, in the way she spoke to him. She wasn't quieter, exactly; rather her drive was more gentle, less demanding. She seemed quicker to fall into enjoyment, even pleasure, and this offered Fechner a route too.

They sat down with Buchanan and one of his colleagues.

'This is Martin,' Buchanan introduced him. 'Martin, Katherine. And this is my friend James.'

They shook hands.

'James?' said Martin. 'James Fechner?'

'Yes,' said Fechner.

'I've heard of you.'

'Is that right?' said Fechner.

'The best surgeon this side of the Boyne, they say.'

'Present company excepted,' said Buchanan.

Fechner smiled. 'Don't you believe it.'

'He is much too modest,' said Katherine. 'I'm working on him.'

Buchanan threw Fechner a look, which Fechner ignored. They made small talk, enjoyed the waning evening sun. When their drinks were done, Fechner went to replenish. As he refilled their glasses, Murphy walked up.

'James,' he said, 'it's good to see you.'

'Is it?' said Fechner.

'Water under the bridge,' he said. 'I hope you hold no ill feelings.'

'Is that right?'

'I wouldn't want anything to damage our professional relationship, is what I mean.'

Fechner said nothing, slowly poured the wine. When he finished he set the bottle on the table, picked up the four glasses. He turned to Murphy.

'I hold no grudges,' he said.

'Good, good,' the big man mumbled.

'But if you ever get in my way again I will teach you what damage means.'

Instinctive, Murphy took a step back.

Fechner smiled. He returned to the table, distributed the glasses.

'Isn't this just a lovely evening,' he said. 'Isn't it just the loveliest.'

Katherine moved back in in September. Their first night in the house together they made love. She lay in his arms afterwards. There was an ease again that surprised both of them. Appetite too. Miles Davis played on the bedside speaker, 'Blue in Green'.

'Where have you been?' Katherine said.

'What do you mean where have I been, I haven't been anywhere.'

She reached up and touched him on the head. 'I mean here. Where have you been in here? I can tell you've been somewhere.'

'I got lost for a little while, just.'

'And did you find yourself again?'

'Who knows,' said Fechner. 'Maybe I did after all.'

In the morning they went to St George's Market for breakfast. She took his hand as they stepped inside. They strolled the aisles, looking first at the art stalls, the jewellery, the second-hand books. Fechner cast an eye over the LPs but saw nothing he wanted.

'How about some food?' he said. 'I'm starving.'

'Doctor.'

Katherine turned around.

'Doctor! Fechner!' The voice louder the second time.

Fechner turned around. Across the aisle, at a stall serving breakfast baps and burgers, stood Lenny and Polio. 'Dunn's Buns' read the sign. Fechner froze. Katherine moved towards them. She had Fechner's hand still so he went too.

'I thought that was you,' said Lenny. He wore a wry expression, like a child who'd just been told the truth about Santa. Polio stood beside him, staring.

'And who is this?' Katherine said, smiling.

'This is Lenny,' said Fechner. 'And Paul. This is my wife, Katherine.'

'I would shake your hand but,' said Lenny. He gestured at the meat surrounding him. 'I've heard all about you.'

'Oh you have, have you?' said Katherine.

'Though you're even more beautiful than he said.'

Katherine laughed.

'How are you keeping, James? Haven't seen you in the shop in a while.'

'I'm well, thank you.'

'And your father?'

Fechner smiled. Lenny was good. 'He's hanging in there.'

Lenny nodded. 'Fair enough.'

'You all right yourself, Paul?' said Fechner.

Polio nodded. 'I'm all right aye.'

'That's good to hear.'

Polio smiled. 'Yes.'

A brief, awkward silence descended.

'Well, if you ever need a good cut of beef you know where to find us,' Lenny said.

'I do,' said Fechner.

'Are the regulars doing all right?' said Fechner.

'They are. They're doing very well indeed.'

'That's good to hear.'

A customer sauntered up, ready to order.

'Well, it was a pleasure to meet you Katherine.'

'Likewise,' she said.

They drifted off towards the other food stalls.

'Is that where you got your meat when you were staying at your father's?' said Katherine.

'That's right,' said Fechner. 'Good butcher he is too.'

'Quite a character, isn't he? Some face. Belfast rarely disappoints on that front.'

13

Joanna loitered on the wall opposite the hospital entrance, jacket pulled tight against the frigid air. It was a grey, murky afternoon in November, sky thick with drizzle. How long had she been sitting there? Fechner spotted her as he stepped through the sliding doors, wondered if he'd time yet to turn and disappear inside. He didn't. She looked up and clocked him.

Fechner ambled towards her. 'Joanna,' he said. 'What brings you here?'

'Where have you been?'

Fechner swept his arm around. *Behold my world.*

'For six months?' Joanna eyed him coolly. 'Do they lock you up at night?'

'People keep getting sick.'

An ambulance sped out of the bay, howling. Fechner watched it go.

'Next weekend is Robert's birthday. We're having a party at ours on Saturday night. Just the usual suspects, low key. It would be good if you could come.'

'Did he send you?'

Joanna laughed. 'Nobody sends me anywhere.'

Fechner said nothing.

'So, will you come?'

'I'm back together with Katherine,' he said. 'My wife. We have plans for Saturday I'm afraid.'

'Lenny told me. I was glad to hear it. You're a man who needs a woman's touch.'

Fechner smiled.

'Well,' she said. 'If anything changes. You know where we are. You still remember, yes?'

'Yes,' said Fechner. 'Yes, I remember.'

Fechner remembered all right. He remembered everything. Images played with such repeated insistence in his mind he could have closed his eyes and painted them. He remembered with precision the days after the incident, the event. Committing to the old routine, sweating it out, pounding heavy on the slick, indifferent machines. *Pounding* the word: he ran like he was being chased.

Young women pass, stare at him. He doesn't see them. He sees himself, returning from the medical cabinet in Blair's office with towels, cotton swabs, gauze pads, Avitene. Helping Rusting up on to one of the benches, carefully shifting him around. Rusting silent save for his heavy, rasping breath. His back sings raw, brutal. Fechner expects him at any moment to refind his function, his faculty, to turn around and grab him and inflict the necessary pain. So be it.

'I'm sorry Robert, but this is going to hurt. Are you ready?'

Rusting gives the tiniest nod, an assent. Fechner holds Rusting's shoulder with one hand, and with the other begins to wash his wounds. Rusting winces, gasps.

'I know, I'm sorry,' Fechner says.

Rusting reaches up, touches Fechner's steadying hand. Fechner holds his breath. As he works on Rusting, an awful, terrifying sympathy grips him, sweeps through him. He goes on, cleans up the blood, tends the bruises and marks, stretches strips across the gashes to hold the skin together. Rusting's breathing slowly steadies, but he says nothing. Still his hand rests on Fechner's. Still Fechner waits for the turn, the seizing, the punishment. Still his heart aches with weakness, with affection, with disgust.

'That's you now,' he says, finally. Rusting sits there, facing away from him, silent. Fechner shivers. He tries to take his hand back from Rusting's shoulder, but Rusting grips it tight. He feels the thudding drub of Rusting's heart rumble through him, reverberating against his own. The rhythm steadies, slows, and then comes the shudder of Rusting's terror, and his quiet, ruthless sobs, spilling out of him with brutal insistence. Fechner feels Rusting's attempt to hold them in, the restraint he tries to force, but his body wins, and out they pour, all the tiny ruptures of anger and grief and hurt and something deeper still, something underneath them all, beyond the reach of anything but tenderness.

Saturday evening. Katherine is working a late shift, won't be home until two in the morning. Fechner fusses on his shirt. He sucks a whisky, combs and recombs his hair. He pours another shot as he waits on the taxi. No harm the pulse moving. The alcohol, caramel and sweet in his mouth, stings on the way down, fizzes through him.

The car drops him a few blocks away, and he walks in anonymous conviction, just to get a feel, some heat in his blood. Clouds hide an insistent moon, a voyeur. He shivers, spits ghosts into the cold night.

The offie is one shop in a dour line of dilapidation. The others are all closed already – a dry cleaner's, a hardware store, a newsagent's. A group of teenagers, maybe fifteen or sixteen years old, linger at the entrance.

'Are you going in there mister?' one of them says.

Fechner hesitates. 'I am yes.'

'Will you get us something? We'll give you the money.'

'No.'

'Fucksake just do it,' another one says. He steps towards Fechner, menacing. He holds out a fiver. 'Some vodka just.'

Fechner stares at the money. A thought takes him, almost by surprise. He reaches out and snatches the note, and steps inside the shop.

He stares at the shelves, considering. Deciding. He feels himself watched by the owner, realises he is grinning dumbly. He selects a bottle of decent wine, carries it over to the counter. As the man rings it up, Fechner points to the shelf behind him.

'A bottle of Glen's too.'

'Did them ones outside put you up to this?'

'Up to what?' Fechner says.

'Are you buying this for those kids?'

Fechner stares at him. 'Do I look like the kind of man who buys drink for kids?'

The man shakes his head. 'It's just—'

'Should I go somewhere else to get what I need?' Fechner says.

'No, no. Sorry.'

The man rings up the total. Fechner pays. He picks up the bottles and turns towards the door.

He can change his mind yet. Well, maybe he can and maybe he can't.

He drops his own bottle into his deep coat pocket, holds the vodka in his hand as he pushes out of the shop. He walks round the corner. The boys are waiting.

'He fucken did too,' the ugly one says.

Fechner holds a finger up. 'What do you say?'

'Give us it,' the kid says.

'Incorrect,' Fechner says, holding out the bottle.

'Look I gave you the money,' he says, reaching his hand out.

'What do you say,' Fechner says.

'Give us the fucken vodka,' the boy says, and shoves him.

Fechner smiles. He saw on them what he knew they had, what they were holding in, but it's on its way now. He lifts the bottle into the air and hurls it to the ground. It smashes with a beautiful, violent explosion. For a second, they stare, all of them, in shock, in incomprehension. And then, as Fechner knew it would, it comes. The punch lands on Fechner's chin. His head snaps back, a tremendous pain shoots through his jaw up into his ears. Another punch catches him in the midriff, and he crumples forwards, on to the ground. Then come the kicks. One arm, instinctive, goes around his head, the other to his stomach, fending off their blows as best he can, but on and on they come, and the pain is so pure and visceral and enveloping he wonders how he'd never known it before. They don't speak, they just kick and kick, and then the door to the shop bells open, and the owner appears, holding a cricket bat. They sprint off, hurling curses as they go. The man watches them, careful, making sure they are really going, but they are, as Fechner knew they would.

'Are you all right?' the man says.

Fechner tries to sit up. The pain is astounding.

'Wait, let me call the police,' the man says.

'No, it's all right,' said Fechner. 'Just help me up would you.'

The man gets him upright and then slowly, his shoulder under Fechner's armpit, drags him up on to his feet. He leans against the wall.

'Look at the state of you,' the man says.

'Me? I'm okay,' Fechner says. He pulls a handkerchief out, dabs at his face. It reddens quickly. Fechner smiles. The pain begins to spread, dissipate into numb coalition, occupying him with a strange, familiar calmness.

'I'll call an ambulance,' the man says.

'Listen to me,' Fechner says, 'I'm all right.'

He feels the man stare at him with hesitation, then suspicion.

'I appreciate your help, but you can go now.'

Fechner nods towards the door. The man stares.

'Go on,' Fechner says.

He shakes his head and steps back inside the shop.

Fechner stands there, slows his breathing down. The freezing air tears at his lungs; his bruised ribs sting. But God, to be alive. He moves off, slowly, back in the direction he'd come, away from where the teenagers scarpered. His left calf aches from the kicking, throbs into a limp. A hundred yards down the road, he stops under a street light by a parked car, examines his face in the window's reflection. Already dark spots flourish. *A geisha*, he thinks, and laughs. He turns his head one way, then the other. He likes what he sees. His hand goes into his pocket. Amazingly, the bottle of wine is intact.

It's a sign, surely. The party awaits. If he cuts through the park and up on to the greenway, he'll be there in ten minutes. He grabs his collar, pulls his coat tight at the neck. Off he sets, hobbling forwards, decisive.

Hold out your arms now, Robert, he thinks. *And see what I do with them.*

Acknowledgements

This book was made possible in part through the support of the Arts Council of Northern Ireland (SIAP Award).

Special thanks to:

Ben Behzadafshar, Chris Fry, Pádraig Ó Tuama and Scott McKendry, for generously reading drafts along the way, and conversations that inspired and challenged.

Rhiannon Smith, Ursula Doyle, Jon Appleton and the team at Fleet, for wise, sharp editing and looking after me during the publishing process.

My agents, Denise Shannon and Judith Murray, for guidance and encouragement throughout. And Toby Moorcroft, keeping his eyes on the big picture.

Myrid Carten, my best critic, creative partner, book titler (Silverback!), lover and wife. *Go raibh maith agat mo chroí.*